Hawley Smart

Beatrice and Benedick

A Romance of the Crimea, Vol. I

Hawley Smart

Beatrice and Benedick
A Romance of the Crimea, Vol. I

ISBN/EAN: 9783743420144

Manufactured in Europe, USA, Canada, Australia, Japa

Cover: Foto ©Andreas Hilbeck / pixelio.de

Manufactured and distributed by brebook publishing software (www.brebook.com)

Hawley Smart

Beatrice and Benedick

BEATRICE AND BENEDICK

A Romance of the Crimea.

BY

H A W L E Y   S M A R T,

AUTHOR OF

"BREEZIE LANGTON," "AT FAULT," "TIE AND TRICK,"
"LONG ODDS," "WITHOUT LOVE OR LICENCE,"
"THE PLUNGER," &c., &c.

IN TWO VOLUMES.

VOL. I.

LONDON :

F. V. WHITE & CO.,
31, SOUTHAMPTON STREET, STRAND, W.C.
1891.

PRINTED BY

KELLY AND CO., GATE STREET, LINCOLN'S INN FIELDS,

AND KINGSTON-ON-THAMES.

CONTENTS.

— ✦ —

TO

HENRY IRVING,

In remembrance of many pleasant nights at the Lyceum, during which the idea of this story first suggested itself, this book is dedicated by his sincere friend and admirer,

HAWLEY SMART.

BEATRICE AND BENEDICK.

A Romance of the Crimea.

———◆———

CHAPTER I.

THE WALKING MATCH.

A BRIGHT sun and a nor'-easter, such as usually characterizes the merry month of May. A white, straight, dusty road, along which a man with his loins girt up and stripped to his shirt and trousers, is walking rapidly and doggedly. He is followed by a little knot of people apparently interested in his proceedings, one of whom, walking by his side, continually consults his watch; indeed, the whole party seem extremely anxious as regards the time. The man, stripped of his coat, looks worn, travel-stained, and bears signs of weariness. If he is walking fast, there can also be little doubt from the set defiant expression in his face that he is walking " in difficulties." From time to time he throws a mute glance at his companion, who usually responds with much the same formula :

" Never fear, old boy — you'll do it all right ; all you have got to do is to keep on walking and think of nothing else. I'm doing *the thinking* for you. You have got a mile to do every fourteen minutes, and you will just win clever ! "

When Hugh Fleming three evenings ago backed himself to walk fifty miles in twelve hours, without training, the whole mess-table laughed. The brother officer who had laid two to one against his doing it, good-naturedly offered to scratch the bet any time during the evening. It seemed perfectly absurd that Fleming should perform any such feat as this. A man who had shown so far not the slightest taste for athletics—who rarely played cricket, never played racquets, and, with the exception of an occasional country walk, for the most part took his exercise round a billiard-table. He had never been known to walk a match, and when this one was made, said that he had never done such a thing before. His comrades all laughed at him, and, with that candour which close intimacy confers, bade him, "Not make a fool of himself, but cry off his bet before it was too late."

There was one exception to the popular feeling—there invariably is—and this was Tom Byng, Fleming's most intimate friend. Byng maintained a rigid silence as to what he thought of the affair, and even when appealed to declined to express any opinion thereon. He was a man who was rather an authority amongst his fellows on all matters of sport, whether with rod or with gun, whether on the race-course or on the cinder-track, and his brother officers were not a little anxious to ascertain what he might

1*

think of this foolish wager. But no, neither at the dinner-table nor in the ante-room afterwards could he be induced to express his views. Until Fleming had retired for the night he smoked silently, and in answer to all inquiries as to what he thought of the match, merely shrugged his shoulders and replied, "I don't know; I never saw him walk in earnest." But no sooner had Fleming retired than, throwing the end of his cigar into the fire, he turned round to the layer of odds and said:

"If you would like to have a little more money against Fleming, Brydon, you can lay me £100 to £50."

"You may put it down," replied the other, "if you will tell me what you are going on."

"Willingly. Unless he is very vain, it is always very dangerous to bet against a man who backs himself, besides, when we were quartered at Portsmouth I once saw Fleming, for a joke, do a thing which, though I be-

lieve no great feat, would puzzle any man
in this room to perform.

"You recollect at one end of the cricket
ground there was a skittle alley, and after
play, or when their side was in, men would
sometimes have a turn at that fine old English game. Precious duffers at it too they
were for the most part. Fleming was in
there one day, chaffing a couple of men who
were playing. When they had finished, he
put up the pins again and said, 'Now if you
fellows can play let's see you take those
down, one pin at a time, that is the nine pins
in nine shots. You mustn't upset two at a
time remember, or you will not have done
what I mean.'

"'Bah,' said one of the men, 'do it, of
course I can't, nor you either. I will lay
you ten to one you can't do it.'

"'I think I can,' replied Fleming quietly,
'although it isn't easy. You *shall* lay me ten
to one in shillings,' and to our astonishment
Fleming proceeded to accomplish the feat.

"I didn't know he could play skittles, and most certainly don't know that he can walk, but he *might*, I'm backing him on the off."

Such were the events which had led up to the match now taking place. Fleming had started at seven in the morning, accompanied only by two brother officers, one of whom was acting as umpire.

When he had accomplished his first twelve miles in two hours and a half and then stopped to breakfast, these gentlemen thought that he would win his wager easily. But the pace was too good to last, and when Byng arrived just as Fleming was finishing his thirtieth mile, the match had begun to look very black for the pedestrian. He was untrained, he had no experience of walking matches, and he had nobody to coach him. Whatever the man's capabilities might be he did not know how to make the most of them. As he had not understood the husbanding of his own powers in the early part of his undertaking, so now he did not know how to use what was left of them. He was losing time on every mile; there were twenty more weary miles to tramp, and each of them took him longer to accomplish than those that had gone before. All the fiery dash of the morning was gone and the afternoon saw the sorely distressed man still struggling gamely with the task which it was rapidly becoming an obvious impossibility that he should perform. Had Byng not arrived at this critical juncture it had been little use his arriving at all; but the minute he understood the state of things he made a rapid calculation in his head, examined Fleming critically as he walked alongside him, and then said:

" I tell you what, old boy; if you're game and will do as I tell you, you will just pull through; but there won't be much to spare."

" I'm about cooked," replied Fleming, " but I'm quite good to go on till you say it's hopeless."

" It's a long way off hopeless at present," replied the other, for the first time giving the advice which he is reiterating at the beginning of this chapter.

As they turned at the milestone (for under Byng's guidance, the mile being tolerably level, the match was to be completed over that mile, walking it backwards and forwards) there was a slight commotion among some of Fleming's partisans, who had now assembled to watch the conclusion of his task. What it was, was hardly discernible at the distance they then were from it, but as they came nearer it was evident that in their zeal for his success some of Fleming's partisans had stopped a smart carriage full of ladies, for fear it should prove a hindrance to their champion. The fair tenants had willingly acquiesced upon understanding what they had to pull up for. Two young ladies stood up as Fleming went by, and scanned him narrowly.

"Who did you say it was, Pritchard?" enquired a tall showy girl, of the coachman.

"It's one of the officers, miss," replied the

man, touching his hat; " but I didn't catch
his name. He's backed himself to walk a lot
of miles in a certain time."

" They are a new lot, Nell," said the
speaker; " they only came in about six or
seven weeks ago. Papa has but just called,
and I haven't met any of them yet. Besides,
you know, in common decency for those who
have gone; the ——th were a very nice lot of
fellows, and very popular; we really must, so
to speak, wear mourning for them a little."

" More than they will do for you, my
dear," replied her companion, laughing.
" Soldiers and sailors are marvellous hands
at quick transfer of the affections."

" Ah, well, I don't suppose there's much
harm done on either side. Singed wings here
and there no doubt, but for most of us only
many a pleasant dancing party to look back
upon, and genuine regret that our pet
partners will meet us no more. This looks
promising for the new comers. As long as a
regiment has some go in them, there's always

hope for us. A very pretty taste in balls and picnics I have noticed often accompanies sporting tendencies, but when we get a regiment that does nothing, as now and again we do—Ugh!" and Miss Smerdon shrugged her pretty shoulders, as much as to say no words could express her feelings for the British soldier who socially failed to do his duty.

A tall, good-looking girl, with a profusion of wavy, brown hair, Miss Smerdon was considered a beauty in her own part of the country. She was the only daughter of a wealthy ironmaster, and in spite of her having two brothers, she was likely, if not an heiress, yet to bring her husband a very substantial dowry. She was a popular girl, and no one could say that Frances Smerdon was deficient in " go." Elderly ladies sometimes shook their heads over her doings, and whispered " bold and fast " behind their fans; but for all· that there was no real harm in her. She rejoiced in high spirits, and was perhaps a little too given to defy conventionalities, but her escapades when looked into were of a very venial nature, and more prompted by her love of fun than anything else. She enjoyed life keenly, as well she might with both youth and wealth at her call, and threw herself into whatever she was doing with all her heart. How she and Nellie Lynden had become such intimate friends was rather a puzzle to their acquaintance. The latter lived in Manchester, but was in the habit of paying long visits to Monmouthshire, where, some half-dozen miles from Newport, Mr. Smerdon had a handsome country seat.

"No! don't let him drive on, Frances, we are in no hurry, and I want to see that officer come back again. I don't know what he's trying to do, but I am interested in it. I feel sure he will do it whatever it is."

"Stay where you are, Pritchard," replied the other, laughing. "We wish to see a little more of this match."

"Well," she continued, turning to her friend, "Love at first sight we've heard of, but faith at first sight such as yours I have never yet met with. Why such belief in this unknown pedestrian?"

"It's a striking face," rejoined Nell Lynden, "I don't mean a particularly handsome one, but a more resolute bull-dog one I never saw. He was in distress when he passed us, but that man will do the task he has set himself, or drop by the wayside."

And now once more Fleming and his three or four attendants pass close to their carriage. He keeps side by side with his mentor, and there is a set dogged look on his face, which, pale though it is, shows no sign of flinching. He is evidently very nearly done, but there can be little doubt that he will go on to the bitter end, and it is evident to all the lookers-on that Byng has determined he shall. To do the latter justice it is not his own stake on it that he is thinking of, but his blood is up, he has identified himself with his

protégé and he is resolved he shall win.
He has made up his mind to take the last
ounce out of his man just as he would out of
his horse in riding a punishing finish. He
has spared himself not a whit since he came
upon the scene, and has walked sixteen miles
by his friend's side; only four miles more
to go, and if his protégé can but keep at the
pace he's going, the match will be won with
five or six minutes to spare. The excitement
waxes intense as the finish draws near.
Win or lose—it *is* a match, and must be a
very close thing. It takes all Byng can do
to keep his man up to the requisite pace,
and there can be no doubt that, left to himself, Fleming would have imperceptibly
slackened in that matter. It is very hard for
a beaten man to keep both his eye on the
watch and regulate his speed at the same time.
The sympathies of the regiment and even of
the lookers on, who had come out of the
neighbouring town to see the finish of such a
sporting affair, are all with Fleming. The

public always wish success to the man who
backs himself in anything of this sort. It
requires pluck to perform such an arduous
task, and that is a thing which always
enlists the sympathies of Englishmen. Even
Brydon could not resist the excitement.

"Upon my word," he exclaimed as the
last mile but one was begun, "I think he'll
win. It will cost me a couple of hundred if
he does, but I can't help hoping he will.
We don't know much of each other till a
pinch comes that's certain. Who'd have
thought that Hugh Fleming had such stuff
in him?"

But this mile Byng had no little trouble to
get his protégé along. Now and again
Fleming stumbled in his walk. The truth
is he was suffering from one of the most
severe trials to which a man is exposed
in a long walk of this nature. His feet
were giving way, which means that before
long the walk must be reduced to a hobble,
and that to crawl a mile within half-an-hour

will be about all that he can accomplish. He had lost two minutes in spite of Byng's exertions over the last, and there remained to him but eighteen minutes in which to walk the concluding mile.

The young ladies had lingered to see the finish of the match, and as Fleming passed their carriage for the last time with still half-a-mile to get, Nell Lynden turned to her friend and said:

" Now let's go home, Frances. He'll do it; but I wish we hadn't stopped to watch him go by this time. Poor fellow, he is suffering terribly. I could see his lips twitch as he passed us."

They well might, for to say nothing of being dead beat, Hugh Fleming was experiencing the sensations of a cat on hot bricks every time he put his feet to the ground. Pritchard turned his horses round, and in accordance with Miss Smerdon's instructions drove leisurely homewards.

But ere they had gone far the sounds of a

ringing cheer fell faintly on their ears, and told them that Hugh Fleming had won his match. It had been a close shave, but the fifty miles had been completed with two good minutes to spare.

"A fine thing, and a pretty match," said Byng, "but I tell you what, Brydon, if he'd only had a week in which to harden his feet, he'd have won with half-an-hour in hand. If you want your revenge, I'll back him to walk——"

"No you don't," cried the hero of the hour, as his partisans picked him up and carried him to the carriage which was in waiting. "This child has had enough walking to last him his natural life. And he's beginning to think that cavalry is the branch of the service which would suit him best."

CHAPTER II.

NELL LYNDEN's father and Mr. Smerdon had been friends in their school-boy days, at which period the position of Lynden's family was certainly superior to that of the latter's. But both boys had their way to make in the world ; neither had any prospect of succeeding to any fortune from their parents. Robert Lynden went up to London and was speedily lost in the whirlpool of the great city. What became of him, what he did there, nobody knew. For the first year or two that he was in London, they heard from him regularly at home. He had apprenticed himself to a chemist, and entertained serious thoughts of turning to medicine as a profession later on, and to enable him to attend the schools his father volunteered considerable

VOL. I.   2

pecuniary assistance. For a few months young Lynden drew on him steadily for this purpose, then suddenly all communication from him ceased. He not only abstained from writing for money, an exigency apt to ensure punctual correspondence, but he did not write at all. His mother grew very anxious about him, enquiries were set on foot, the chemist to whom he had bound himself was duly communicated with, and replied that Robert Lynden, after voluntarily apprenticing himself, had broken his indentures at the end of a year, and that he had neither seen nor heard anything of him since. His father went up to town and made enquiries in every direction. He even consulted the police on the subject; but no, nothing could be heard of the missing youth, London seemed to have swallowed him up, and all endeavours to ascertain his fate proved useless. He was advertised for in all directions, for his people were well enough to do to be able to spend some little money in trying to trace their boy. But nothing came of enquiry or advertisement, and after a time his mother mourned for him as dead, while his father came sadly to the conclusion that his disappearance was one of those inscrutable mysteries ever characteristic of great cities. Whether he had been foully done to death who could say? or whether he was the unrecognised victim of some accident. But that their son was dead, neither Mr. nor Mrs. Lynden entertained the slightest doubt, and in due course of years went to their graves undisturbed in that belief.

Nellie Lynden could have told you very little about her father's antecedents. She could barely remember her mother, who had died when she was very young, and from that time her life had simply been a progress from one school to another. Clever, sensitive, even as a child the thought had oppressed her that she belonged to nobody. She was kindly treated, but it was bitter for her when the holidays came and the other girls went to

2*

their homes. There were no holidays for her, for what were holidays without a home? and she had no home. Boys we know can be very cruel to each other, and I fancy girls are very little better in this respect. Some of her schoolmates, perhaps because they were out of temper, perhaps from that innate desire to torture which exists in the young of both sexes, would twit Nellie when the holidays came round with having nowhere to go to. They would enquire, with affected interest, if she did not find it dull being there all those weeks by herself. And she did find it dull—horribly dull, and they knew it.

Her school-mistresses were kind enough, but what could they do? Their engagement with her father was that they should always take care of her in the holidays, as he had no home to take her to. He was kind enough to the desolate girl upon his few brief visits, and lavish with regard to money for her dress or anything else she fancied as she grew older. But, except occasionally for a very few days, he had never taken her away with him. And then an hotel had been her home. The result of this peculiar training had been to make Nellie Lynden a somewhat reserved girl, not one to give away her friendship lightly, and though popular in every school she had ever been in, she had never formed one of those gushing friendships which girls are so apt to contract in these days.

Some four years before our story commences she had been called upon to come home and take charge of her father's house. For the first time in his life Dr. Lynden admitted of having a house. Nellie further wondered on the receipt of this letter, whether he had also a practice. Questioned once upon this point, he had replied that he had practised chiefly abroad, that he had given it up now, and only prescribed in an amateurish way for a few intimate friends and acquaintances. He had further made some rather severe strictures on the vice

of curiosity, and avowed his opinion that
there was no such bore alive as a painfully
inquisitive person. This was quite sufficient
hint for Nellie. She never ventured to
inquire further into the past life of her
father. She accepted things as they were,
and admitted that she had no cause to
complain. The doctor's house in the suburbs
of Manchester, though not large, was extremely comfortable. Nellie was perfectly
satisfied with the rooms placed apart for her
exclusive use, as well as the drawing-room
and dining-room. The doctor reserved for
himself besides his bed-room, a large room
fitted up as a laboratory, which he called
his "den." The peculiarity about this room
was that it was guarded by elaborate double
doors from the rest of the house, and further,
had a separate stair communicating with the
outside, so that it was possible for the
doctor from his laboratory to leave the house
without the knowledge of the other inmates.
The outer of these doors was kept jealously

locked, which the doctor explained by saying
that evil smells were emitted from apartments
of that description, and that he did not wish
the rest of the house poisoned ; moreover that
servants could never resist touching things,
and that he did not wish a housemaid to blow
her head off by fiddling with a retort which
did not concern her. He had had a passion
for chemistry from his youth up, but it was
really only of late that he had found leisure
to indulge it.

"I can't say as yet, Nell, that I've made
any discovery calculated to benefit mankind.
I don't suppose I ever shall, but it amuses
me, and hurts nobody. I've done my best to
render my hobby inoffensive, so you must put
up with it."

" My dear father," said Miss Lynden, " why
shouldn't you do as you like in your own
house ? As for the laboratory, the double
doors are so effective that 1 am sure no one
could ever detect that there was such a
thing in the place."

If Dr. Lynden went out but little himself he was not forgetful of his daughter. He made arrangements with a lady, with whose husband he was tolerably intimate, to act as Nell's chaperon, and as that young lady herself was by no means unattractive, she was not long before she knew a good many people in Manchester. Her chaperon, Mrs. Montague, was one of those vivacious ladies who contemplate passing an evening at home with dismay. This restless lady could not bear the idea of not assisting at everything that was going on in Manchester, and would work with untiring patience and assiduity to obtain tickets. The more difficult they were to come by, I verily believe the more she enjoyed it, and she was perfectly callous to all social rebuff in matters of this nature.

Some two years ago, Nellie, while under the wing of Mrs. Montague, chanced to meet Frances Smerdon at a dinner-party, and the ironmaster's daughter at once conceived a strong liking for the quiet, reticent, lady-like girl. Miss Smerdon, who had come on a month's visit to Manchester, contrived to see a good deal of her new friend in the course of her visit. In the first instance the liking had been entirely on the part of Frances, but gradually Nellie thawed under the advances of her more impressionable friend, and before Miss Smerdon left, it had been arranged that Nellie should pay her a visit in Monmouthshire. Dr. Lynden, as soon as he knew who she was, took the greatest possible interest in Miss Smerdon. He enquired after her father, whom he recollected as the employé of a great iron company in South Wales, and seemed much struck at discovering that he had blossomed into a large ironmaster on his own account. Although reticent about his own past as ever, he told Frances that he and her father had been school-fellows, and this seemed an additional link in the friendship of the two girls. It had subsisted now about two years, and Frances was enthusiastic in Miss Lynden's praises.

Knowing her father's strong opinions on the sin of curiosity, Nellie was rather amused to see how extremely interested he was in all particulars concerning the life of his old chum, Matthew Smerdon. He never wearied of asking Smerdon's daughter about him on such occasions as Frances was in Manchester, and cross-examined Nellie on her return from Monmouthshire in a manner diametrically opposed to his expressed opinions. Smerdon too, in his turn, had been curious to hear of his old school-boy friend, and the two girls sometimes discussed their respective fathers, but there was this difference, whereas Matthew Smerdon's career was not only well-known to his daughter but to all his neighbours, from the very outset, nobody knew anything about Dr. Lynden's, from his disappearance almost as a boy in the great London wilderness, until his reappearance as a retired medical man in Manchester some four years ago. That he had practised on the Continent, and made money, was the brief account that Dr. Lynden deigned to give of his past.

  *   *   *   *   *

At this particular juncture there commenced a bickering between England and the great Autocrat of the North, which, little as anyone dreamed of it at the time, was shortly destined to set all Europe by the ears. Europe had been at peace ever since Waterloo, and that big battles were ever again to be fought amongst the western nations was apparently looked upon by politicians with incredulity. Still that real or mythical will of Peter the Great had always been kept steadily in sight by the rulers of Russia. To come to Constantinople sooner or later ever their fixed resolution, and the Turks still believe just as firmly that they will, and that it is their *Kismet*. But as to about the when they are to arrive there the Russians have fallen into great mistakes. If the Turk submits resignedly to his *Kismet* in the end, yet he will fight bitterly to avert it, as he has

shown at Plevna and elsewhere. Moreover
the nations of Europe have ever regarded
with jealous eyes the idea of Russia at
Constantinople. The Czar, Nicholas, was
doubtless aware of all this when he made up his
mind that the pear was ripe for the plucking.
Europe might not like it, but who was there
to interfere with him? There was no united
Germany in those days. France had only
recovered from its state of chronic revolution
to have a relapse in the shape of a *coup-d'etat*,
while for England one might as well expect
to see a Quaker in the prize ring as Great
Britain intervening by arms in any of the
quarrels of Europe.

The nations of the West might not like it;
but then in the words of the immortal Wegg,
" The nations of the West were at liberty to
lump it." Very busy was the English Government with notes, and protests, circulars, etc.,
finally dabbling with that most dangerous of
all documents, an ultimatum. That England
would ever fight about such a trifle as Russia

annexing the Danubian provinces of Turkey was a thing neither believed in by the Czar nor the British Government. But the temper of the English people had to be reckoned with. The English people may be thickheaded, but they are also extremely obstinate, and close on forty years ago John Bull made up his mind that he would stand no Russian aggression, and that it was his bounden duty to protect the Turks. After Waterloo, the Millennium; forty years, and there comes another big war; forty years again, and those gallant Turks for whom it was waged are pronounced "unspeakable." And I fancy there are a good many big battles yet to be fought before we come to the final field of Armageddon.

The English nation had taken the bit between its teeth, and was " neither to haud nor to bind." It was bent upon fighting, and no Government could control it—kicked the Government of the day indeed out of the saddle in a very short time. Whether we

were ready for war, or indeed whether any
nation in Europe was what would be termed
ready for war in these days, is open to question. Before we knew where we were, we
were committed to it, and had to make the
best of it. That this should occasion much
confusion at the Horse Guards, as it was then,
and much ordering and counter-ordering of
troops, was only natural. One thing which
still further complicated affairs was the per-
sistency with which the Government clung to
the belief that the whole thing would end after
all in " a demonstration," that the strengthen-
ing of our garrisons in the Mediterranean and
the landing of a small army at Gallipoli must
convince the Czar that we were in earnest.
It was not likely that the proud ruler of the
hordes of Turkestan and the Steppes of
Tartary would flinch from lifting the gauntlet
we had thrown down, and of this our rulers
were very shortly destined to be convinced.

Now all this led, of course, to much shifting
and changing of troops, the places of regiments

that had been promptly shipped off to the East had to be filled by others, brought from wherever the authorities could lay hands on them. Our military chiefs were painfully cognisant that they could do with many more regiments than we actually possessed, and that the British Army was terribly small in comparison to all that was required of it. Regiments got shuffled about in rather higgledy-piggledy fashion in those days. One thing safe to keep clearly in mind, that wherever a regiment might be sent it was as well it should be handy to a port of embarkation, for it was patent to anyone that if there was really going to be war every soldier that could be laid hands on in the United Kingdom would be required on the scene of action. The result of all these changes was that Her Majesty's —th found themselves, much to their disgust, in Manchester one fine day, having been sent there to relieve a regiment told off for the East.

Miss Smerdon, who happened to be staying

with the Lyndens, picked up the news in the course of her morning walk. Nearly a year had elapsed since the great walking match, and Frances Smerdon had seen a good deal of the —th since then, but it so happened Miss Lynden had not. She had paid one short visit in the autumn, but the only one of the officers from Newport she had met during that time was Captain Byng. Frances laughed at the time, and said, " It's not my fault, Nell, I assure you we asked your hero to dinner, but he's away on leave somewhere, and I could not catch him."

" Oh, you may laugh at my hero," rejoined the girl gravely, " but they will all have a chance of being heroes shortly."

" Why, nobody thinks there is going to be a war, really," exclaimed Miss Smerdon.

" Oh, yes, Frances, they do. My father does for one. He not only thinks there'll be war, but a big war too."

" But even if there should be, the —th are not under orders for it, and I hope they won't

be. I don't want to think my friends, my
partners, men whose hands have only lately
pressed mine, are carrying their lives in their
hands."

" They'd not thank you for wishing them
out of it," cried Miss Lynden as her eyes
sparkled. " Didn't you hear that spirited
new song the other night, ' Boot and saddle,
the pickets are in,' how the officer who sang it
gave out the line, ' And we're not the lads to
leave out of the dance.' I can understand
a soldier would feel that ; however, your
Newport friends needn't fret. If war is really
meant, as my father thinks, he says none of
the soldiers need trouble themselves about
their not going out, they will all find themselves there before long."

" Ah well, I can only hope Dr. Lynden's
wrong," said Miss Smerdon, " and now give
me some lunch, for I am nearly starving."

CHAPTER III.

MISS SMERDON had become a great favourite
with the Doctor, and his daughter would often
say jestingly that Frances could turn him
round her finger. Indeed, Nellie sometimes
affected to be jealous, and declared that she
believed her friend would wind up by becoming her mamma. This, however, was the
merest badinage, still the young lady was
undoubtedly a great favourite with the Doctor,
and could coax him into pretty nearly what
she pleased. On one point only was the
Doctor inflexible ; he would not show her
what she denominated " Blue Beard's chamber." She had asked to see it in the first
instance in the idlest spirit of curiosity. It
was a wet day. She felt dull, or something
of that sort. The Doctor parried her request

in good-humoured fashion. He read her a lecture on the sin of being inquisitive, but he did not show her his den. This only stimulated the girl's desire to see the inside of the laboratory. She returned to the charge again and again, and though Frances was always assured the Doctor could refuse her nothing, she discovered that he could, and most decidedly too. Frances Smerdon said nothing; she did not even tell her friend, but she registered a vow in her own breast that if she ever did get the opportunity, she would investigate the laboratory pretty thoroughly. She questioned Nellie as to whether she had ever been inside it, and the girl's reply was only once, and then for a very few minutes. " I never was in any other laboratory, but I suppose they are all much alike. A sort of cooking-range, a small furnace, and all sorts of queer-shaped glass bottles."

Miss Smerdon considered. She also had never seen a laboratory.

" I recollect," she murmured, " hearing a

3*

gentleman say, it was with regard to invitations, that he always went everywhere he was asked, once, on the same principle that you should see everything once, of course, therefore it's my business to see a laboratory once if I can." However an opportunity to get inside the Doctor's den did not seem likely to present itself. ·She had coaxed him, and pledged herself not to be frightened at anything she might see inside, even skeletons; but it was no use : the Doctor was inflexible. She enquired of Nellie if anybody was ever admitted there.

" A few pupils of chemistry who come to him from the outside and whom I never see, and also Phybbs the housemaid, but Phybbs' visits are rare, and are only made under my father's immediate superintendence."

From that instant Phybbs became invested with considerable interest in the eyes of Miss Smerdon, as one versed in the Asian mysteries. She even condescended to converse with Phybbs on the subject, which was·

quite contrary to Miss Smerdon's usual
habits, as though considerate she was given
to keeping a stiff upper lip with servants.
It was odd that her curiosity should be so
excited about such a trifle, but she was
a rather spoilt young woman, accustomed to
have her own way in everything, and moreover it is just about these very trifles we do
become so painfully exercised. What she
had gathered from Nellie and Phybbs ought
to have satisfied her, but it did not. The
doctor spent a great deal of his time in his
laboratory, and Frances Smerdon pictured
him as perpetually transmuting baser metals
into gold, seeking for the philosopher's stone,
or indulging in the darker mysteries of the
Rosicrucians. Who were these pupils that
Nellie spoke of? Disciples, of course, she
ought to have called them; for, gifted with a
vivid imagination, Miss Smerdon was rapidly
investing the doctor with supernatural
powers, and believing him to be the head
of a sect. She was a girl with a very

romantic kink in her brain, and had built all these visions in her own mind on the plain prosaic fact that her host was an elderly gentleman, who dabbled in chemistry, and did not want his retorts and crucibles meddled with.

However, Miss Smerdon had not much time to indulge in further imaginings. The embarkation of the troops caused a feeling through England that she did not perhaps make enough of her soldiers. If we were going to war—and practical people said we were virtually at war at that very time, although perhaps not a shot would be fired— still it behoved the nation to send forth her army handsomely. There might be bitter tears to shed, even over victories, should real fighting ever begin; but at the present moment there was a deal of "Rule Britannia" about, "Britons never, never shall be slaves," and all that sort of thing. It was right that our young heroes should be feasted before going into the lists—destined to be heroes in real earnest too, whether in life or death, many of them. But all this was in futurity. At present the banners waved, the bands played, the crowd cheered, the officers dined and danced, and war was apparently one of the most light-hearted of pastimes. There had been much talk of giving a great ball to the regiment which the —th had relieved, but soldiers get scant warning on these occasions, and unfortunately the proposed guests were packed off to the East a little before the date fixed for the entertainment. " What was to be done? " said the committee. " We have excited society in Manchester, and society must be satisfied. Postpone the ball we may, to put it off altogether is impossible." Then arose in that committee a hard practical man, who opined that one regiment was as good as another—in his heart he considered they were all expensive encumbrances. As long as the Manchester ladies got their ball, they would be content. As long as their partners have red coats, girls don't trouble their heads about who is inside of them. Ask the new regiment instead of the old, it will all come to the same thing. And so it came about that no sooner had they appeared in Manchester than the —th found themselves fêted in all directions. It was necessary, of course, to make the acquaintance of the new-comers before this ball, given in their honour, took place. The young ladies of the city were most positive on this point, and the result was the humblest subaltern of the —th found himself committed to as many engagements as in these days falls to the lot of an African explorer.

"I tell you what, old man," exclaimed Byng, as he lounged in the ante-room one morning after parade, "it's well for you that you hadn't two or three weeks in Manchester before you backed yourself for your big walk. They can't mean us for active service, or they would never have sent us to such a Capua as this. Last night's the fifth night I've dined out this week. Do you? Well, if turtle, champagne, punch——"

"Are little comforts you will find the Government don't provide on active service," exclaimed Fleming laughing.

"No," returned the other. "By-the-way, I took in to dinner a very nice-looking girl, who manifested an undue interest in your unworthy self—Miss Lynden."

"Don't know her — never even heard of her," replied Hugh Fleming sententiously.

"Well, you needn't crow, young man. She never saw you but once, and whatever you may think of your personal appearance, you weren't looking your best then."

"When was that?" asked Hugh.

"She saw you finish your match," replied Byng. "Didn't look much of it myself just then, but you — a shambling broken-down tramp was the only possible description of you."

"Don't be personal, man," rejoined Hugh. "I've a hazy recollection of passing a carriage with some ladies in it. I wonder how she knew my name?"

"Oh, she was staying with the Smerdons. She often stays with them, and you were a local celebrity for a few days, remember. Miss Smerdon was there last night. Everyone was raving about this ball. I tell you what, my children," continued Byng, addressing the little knot of officers in the ante-room, "soldiers are up, they've touched about the top price they've ever been at since I've been in the service. Manchester is popularly supposed to abound in heiresses—obvious deduction. Take advantage of your opportunities, and bless you, etc." And here Byng extended his hands after the manner of the conventional stage father.

The evening of the ball arrived. It really had aroused great enthusiasm. Romantic young ladies declared it put them in mind of the Duchess of Richmond's famous ball at

Brussels the night before Waterloo, looked up "Childe Harold," and quoted :

"There was mounting in hot haste."

But these were the exception. Generally the younger portion of the community looked forward to a capital dance, and the elder to a capital supper. Miss Smerdon and Nellie were of course there under the charge of Mrs. Montague, and Miss Smerdon was most thoroughly mistress of the situation. Not only had Mrs. Montague a large acquaint-ance, but Frances was well known and popular with the officers of the —th. The two girls were speedily in great request, and it was not long before Miss Smerdon brought up Hugh Fleming to be introduced to her friend.

"Capital ball, Miss Lynden," said Fleming, as he led her away to join the dancers, "but Manchester strikes me as having gone mad. The whole thing seems so utterly unreal. I can't help feeling that I'm the shallowest of impostors."

"I don't understand you," said the girl.

"What I mean is this," said Fleming, "Manchester is fêting us, dining us, giving us this ball, all just as if we'd done something. Not only we haven't, not only we never may, but we may never even have the chance. I always feel that I'm dining out under false pretences."

"Very proper of you to say so, but you're wrong all the same. I'll admit that in a vulgar sense, you are discounting your laurels before you've won them, but you will have your opportunity before long, and English women have no doubt about English soldiers winning the bays when the chance comes."

"Very prettily put, Miss Lynden, but you may do any amount of hard fighting without distinguishing yourself."

"You're a little selfish, Mr. Fleming," said the young lady smiling. "As the individual, yes; as a regiment, no; and you soldiers are very proud of the corps to which you belong, are you not?"

" Yes, there are two things a man seldom loses his sympathy for, his old school, and his old regiment. While he's in it, it's the one regiment."

" Yes, I've seen enough of you military men to know that."

" One of our weaknesses," laughed Fleming, as he put his arm round her waist and whirled her off to the inspiriting strains of " The Sturm Marsch."

Nell Lynden was looking extremely well that evening. If not a pretty girl, she was at all events a decidedly attractive one, as with dark chestnut hair, bright hazel eyes, good teeth, and a neat figure, she could not well help being.

She was not accomplished, but there were some two or three things that Nell could do to perfection. Her waltzing was the poetry of motion. She had not much voice, but to hear her warble an old English ballad, in those low contralto tones of hers, would stir most men's pulses. She was a very self-reliant girl, partly by nature, but still more so by her bringing up. She had never met with ill-treatment or unkindness, but for all that she had always regarded herself as a friendless little Arab, with only herself to depend upon. Indeed Frances Smerdon was the only intimate friend of her own sex she had ever made ; and there was one side of Frances' character which she was incapable of understanding, and that was the imaginative side of her disposition. People of this very sanguine temperament can never control themselves, nor even in old age utterly abandon the habit. They build their castles in the air on the largest scale and upon the slenderest foundations, and constantly as these Chateaux d'Espagne come tumbling about their ears they are neither discouraged nor disconcerted.

" Well, Miss Lynden," said Fleming, as, their valse finished, he took his charge back to her chaperone, " I hope your prophecy may prove true—that we shall have the opportunity of winning our laurels before the year's out, and also that individually I shall be quick enough to snatch at mine when the chance comes."

"You've got one grand quality for a soldier, Mr. Fleming," replied the girl, laughing—"dogged pertinacity. You would never have won that walking match if you hadn't. It would be hard to convince you that you were beaten, about anything."

"I don't like giving in," replied Hugh.

"Neither do I," returned the girl. "We are both what our friends, Mr. Fleming, call obstinate."

That the war should be the ruling topic of conversation was inevitable. A considerable part of the English people still found it difficult to believe that we really were at war —destined to remain in that belief too, for some months to come. The men of that time knew from their fathers how England had rung with the news of victories, when the century was young, and fully expected news of a great battle before six weeks were over. But things are not done quite so quickly as all that. Where to bring off a fight, used to be a knotty problem in the latter days of the prize-ring, and this was just the point which at the present moment puzzled our rulers. Russia vaguely told us to come on, but had inconsiderately forgotten to name where the combat was to take place.

Miss Smerdon, as we know, had no belief that there would ever be actual hostilities, and she was rather chaffing Byng on obtaining hospitality under false pretences, indeed it really was a joke in the regiment at their being fêted, mainly because their predecessors had been sent campaigning.

"Ah, you can chaff us, Miss Smerdon," said Byng, "but we really have a good deal the best of the joke; you see we've got the cakes and ale, and may never gather the laurels."

"There, never mind the war," replied Frances, "let's talk about something else.

You know Miss Lynden, you've met her at our house."

"Certainly," rejoined Byng; "not a girl one is at all likely to forget."

"Have you ever met Doctor Lynden?"

"Only once, and that was at a small bachelor dinner, and how I was included in that to the present moment I can't imagine. They were a scientific lot, and how they came to think that a Captain of Infantry was a savant, I can't conceive."

"Now tell me all about it, Captain Byng. This interests me."

"More than it did me," rejoined the soldier. "They talked a good deal about things a little over my head. Nothing for it but the old magpie dodge, you know. I didn't talk much, but I thought the more. I know I got through no end of claret."

"Nonsense, Captain Byng, you must know what they talked about, and I particularly want to know."

"Well, chemical discoveries, new beliefs, and all sorts of things you never hear at a mess-table. Blest if I don't think everyone of the party had a religion of his own——"

"Except yourself," said Miss Smerdon, sweetly, "but you surely can recollect some of the talk if you try, Captain Byng."

"Indeed, I can't, my sole recollection of that evening was, that it was dull, that the claret was good, and that I was there by mistake."

"It's very provoking. You know I am staying here with the Lyndens. The Doctor is a charming old man, but I'm dreadfully curious about him."

"Clever old fellow," replied Byng, "they're all too clever for me, but I'm bound to say I don't think Dr. Lynden would have gone on propounding his rigmarole theories if the others had left him alone."

"I only wish I had had half your opportunity," rejoined Miss Smerdon. "Now take me back to Mrs. Montague, please, for it's getting late, and I daresay she's wanting to go home."

Byng did as he was bid, and as he wished his fair partner " good night," marvelled much in what way he had missed his opportunity. It was impossible for him to know the theory that Miss Smerdon's vivid imagination had conceived concerning her host, and that she regarded Captain Byng as having been present at a secret conclave of adepts in mysticism.

4*

CHAPTER IV.

CONSTABLE TARRANT.

"You see, Pollie, I'm a man of intellect, that's what I am. I may be only an ordinary police-constable now, but my chance will come, and then you'll see a lot about this 'active and intelligent officer,' and all the other clap-trap."

"Of course you are, Dick, everybody knows you are awfully clever," and Miss Phybbs looked admiringly at the sandy-haired young man in a policeman's uniform with whom she was walking.

Constable Tarrant looked at her suspiciously for a moment. He was quite aware his talents were not so universally admitted as Polly suggested. But he was a young man with a very excellent opinion of himself, and though, during the two years he had been in

the force, nothing had taken place to afford
any grounds for the belief, he was certainly
firmly impressed with the idea that he was
destined to achieve greatness in the career
upon which he had embarked. Polly Phybbs
was a thin-lipped, black beady-eyed young
woman, a trustworthy capable servant and
with no weakness about her excepting her
love for this cousin of hers, Richard Tarrant.
Whatever he said was law to her. She was
four or five years his senior, and he had
made love to her from the time he was fifteen,
not very disinterested love either, for from the
very commencement he had utilised her in
every possible way. He invested her with
the general supervision of his wardrobe, let
her wait upon him, and work for him, and
spent a considerable portion of her wages for
her to boot. A sharp, hard-working girl, she
was never long out of a good situation, and
might by this have saved money if it had
not been for her infatuation for her cousin;
shrewd though she was on all other matters,

on this point she was blind. Though a smart-looking girl with a rather neat figure, nobody could call her good-looking. It might be that she attracted no other sweetheart, but certain it is that she had been for the last seven or eight years completely devoted to Richard Tarrant. When after having failed twice or thrice in his attempts to get a living, Dick succeeded in getting into the police force, she quite believed that it was due to the display of considerable talent on his part, and felt quite sure that he would sooner or later distinguish himself. She was not pledged to be married to him, but he was her young man, and she quite understood that they would be married some of these days—some of these days being interpreted into such time as she should have saved money enough to start housekeeping on.

"Now," said Dick, "you see in my profession"—Police Constable Tarrant was given to speaking grandiloquently of his calling—"a fellow's only got to keep his eyes open, and his turn must come. Now you know, Polly, I always was a regular wonner for observing."

Polly dutifully assented, although she could call to mind no particular recollections of this faculty in her cousin.

"I notice everything. If I see a chap loitering, I says to myself at once: 'Now, what's he loitering for?' He don't gammon me that he's tired and his boots hurt him. 'On you go, my man,' says I. Bless you, he might be keeping watch while two or three of his pals commit a burglary. No, no, my girl, my eye is everywhere, and when your eye's everywhere you're bound—well, you're bound to see something at last," concluded Mr. Tarrant, rather feebly.

It did not occur to Polly that in a big city like Manchester those gimlet eyes of Constable Tarrant's ought, in the course of two years, to have detected crime of some nature. Dick had never told her of any such success, neither had he told her of a pretty sharp

reprimand he had received from his superiors
when a gentleman's watch was snatched
almost under his very nose, without attract-
ing his observation.

"Now," resumed Tarrant, "this master of
yours is a queer sort of a man. What can
he want with a side door to his house? You
see all these villa residences are built exactly
alike, except your house. Now, who is Dr.
Lynden that he should have a side door all to
hisself? That's what I want to know."

"Lor', Dick, my master's as quiet an old
gentleman as you'd meet anywhere; there's
no harm in him."

"That's your unsuspecting nature," replied
the constable, loftily. "The law is suspicious; the police, which is an arm of the
law, is suspicious too—me, I'm suspicious—
it's my duty."

"I tell you what, it's all nonsense your
being suspicious of master; and as for Miss
Lynden, she is as sweet a young lady as
ever I saw——"

"Don't rile me, Polly; you'll make me suspicious of you next. I tell you, sometimes when I've been hanging about here after you, I've seen two or three suspicious characters go in at that side door."

"What do you call suspicious characters, Dick?"

"They were men," replied Constable Tarrant, glaring at his companion in a most Othello-like manner.

"Some of master's chemical friends most likely," suggested Miss Phybbs.

"Friends! Lovers—lovers of yours!" exclaimed Tarrant, with a burst of well-acted jealousy.

"Now, don't be foolish, Dick; you know I care for nobody but you. Men do come in at times by that door to see master. It was built on purpose; they are friends interested in his experiments, and go straight to the chemical room without going through the house."

"Polly," said Tarrant, endeavouring to call

up a look of preternatural sagacity, "your
master's conduct is suspicious. It's your
duty to the public to keep your eye on him.
It's your duty to me to keep your eye on
him."

"I assure you you're all wrong. My
master's a quiet, harmless old gentleman, who
shuts himself in with his pots and pans, and
blows himself up occasionally. I go in now
and then, when he's there, but bless you,
there's nothing to see in the room."

"It's not likely a woman would see anything in it. It would look very different, no
doubt, to a police officer."

"But what is it you suspect the doctor of
doing?"

"That's it," replied Constable Tarrant. "I
suspect him; it doesn't signify what of, at
present. Keep your eye on him, Polly."

Polly laughed as she replied : "Of course I
will, if you tell me to, and now I must run
away. Kiss me, Dick, before I go, and don't
be long before you come and see me again."

And their embrace over, Miss Phybbs sped
home, conscious that she had considerably
exceeded the time for which she had been
granted leave of absence.

"I don't know what he's up to. I don't
know what his little game is, but the circumstances are suspicious," said Mr. Tarrant, as
he walked quickly back to his own dwelling.
"Let's reckon it all up," he continued, stop-
ping and placing the forefinger of his right
hand solemnly on the palm of his left.
" First, you've a doctor with no visible means
of earning his living, verdict on that, rum,
and I only wish I knew how he did it.
Secondly, he has a private room, into which
nobody is ever allowed to go, rummer.
Lastly, he's a private stair, and a private
door, what's he want with a private
door? rummest. Men go in by day, what
goes in by night?" There was a pause
of some seconds, and then Mr. Tarrant
suddenly laid the forefinger of his right
hand against the side of his nose, winked

at an imaginary audience, and ejaculated
" Bodies ! "

*   *   *   *   *

Doctor Lynden meanwhile continues the
harmless tenor of his ·way, dining out occasionally, and for the most part with the
savants of Manchester, among whom he is
now generally well-known. He spends a
good deal of time in his laboratory, in experiments, presumably, the result of which
has not yet been published to the outside
world. That Miss Smerdon has a strong
girlish curiosity to see the inside of his den he
knows, but he little thinks what that imaginative young lady pictures his real life.
Still further would he have been astonished
to hear that a rather thick-headed young
policeman was also taking a lively interest in
his proceedings. At the former he would
probably have only laughed ; but had he
been cognisant of the latter, he would doubtless have been seriously annoyed. Nobody
cares to be under the observation of the

police—the guilty naturally dislike it; the innocent fiercely resent it; but to find one-self under the self-imposed surveillance of a young police constable would exasperate most men. Fortunately for his peace of mind, Doctor Lynden is in blissful ignorance of there even being such a person as Police Constable Tarrant, at present.

But the summer slips away. Miss Smerdon has long ago gone back to her home. The army has moved from Gallipoli to Varna, but still those bulletins of " Glorious victory," for which the British public yearn, are not forth-coming. The cavalry has lost a good many men and horses from an expedition into the unhealthy Dobrutschka, but of actual cross-ing of swords and exchanging shots there has been none ; still rumour has it that both French and English fleets, with innumerable transports, have all been collected at Varna, that such a flotilla has not been seen since the days of the Armada ; and, indeed, that probably would have seemed a very small affair compared to that assembled in the Black Sea under the flags of the allies.

Russia has long ago yielded the naval supremacy, and is destined ere long to make grim reparation to the Turks for Sinope, by voluntarily sinking her own fleet in the mouth of Sebastopol Harbour. That an expedition of some sort has been decided upon, that the combined forces of French and English are about to embark and the war to commence in bitter earnest, is now well-known, though the exact destination of the expedition is kept as secret as possible. But let it land where it will, it will be upon Russian soil, and that a pitched battle will speedily follow, is confidently predicted. This time the Quid Nuncs are right, another week or two, and all England will ring with the victory of the Alma. A little longer, and men will look grimly and women weep over those terrible lists of killed and wounded which inevitably follow all glorious victories. Men think sadly of many a good fellow who

they will never clasp hands with more, and
maidens think sadly of friends who had been
rather more than friends to them but a few
months back; and who they had dreamed
might in the future be something dearer still.
But those who conduct wars have no time for
sentiment; the ravening monster requires
perpetual fresh food for his insatiable maw,
and the sole thought of the authorities is how
the losses are to be made good—how to fill
the places of those who have fallen; and it
is already evident to all military men that
to find the necessary reinforcements will tax
our small army to the utmost. Men who are
fretting their hearts out because they have
been so far " left out of the dance " grow
jubilant. They feel that it cannot be long
now before they are called upon to bear their
part. Then comes the false report of the fall
of Sebastopol, and these restless spirits are
filled with alarm lest the whole thing should
be over without their having anything to do
with it. But that canard is soon exploded,

and when the real state of things becomes
known, England generally awakes to the fact
that this is no military promenade, but that
if she is seeking a big war, she has got it. A
few weeks more, and home comes the story of
Inkermann, and when the bulletins of that
glorious, but grisly battle are read—accounts
of such fierce hand-to-hand fighting as recalled the storming of Badajos, and other
such scenes in the Peninsular war—sensible
men could no longer doubt we were committed to the biggest struggle we had been
engaged in since the Titan was caged at St.
Helena. The country has woke up in earnest
now, and not only is every available soldier
in the United Kingdom hurried to the front,
but from all parts of the Empire, England's
sons are summoned to her aid.

It is needless to say that the ——th had
received marching orders, they were to go
to Malta in the first instance, thence to be
pushed on to the Crimea in the early spring.
Hard-worked and hard-pressed though the

army at the front was, yet the authorities found they were hard put to it to feed it, dreadfully depleted though its ranks were.

Some months had elapsed since that great ball which inaugurated their arrival in Manchester had been given to her Majesty's ——th, and in that time the officers had naturally become intimate with the people of the place. Miss Lynden for instance had become well-known to several of them, but the most persistent visitor at the doctor's house was Hugh Fleming. He made no disguise to himself that he was falling deeply in love. He knew, and if he didn't, it would have been for no want of telling that what his chum, Tom Byng, was continually dinning in his ears was true, that there was no higher pinnacle of folly than the committal of matrimony by a subaltern in the army, that as matters stood at present, all love-making ought to be punished by court-martial; that for a man just going out to fight for his Queen and country, for pay and plunder, for glory and promotion, to be whispering love-speeches was criminal with no extenuating circumstance, and deserved to be met by placing a bandage round the culprit's eyes and interviewing him with a few file of loaded muskets, at the back of the barrack square.

"Why do I tell you all this, young un? Why do I keep pitching into you, d—n it? because you want it! You're getting spoons, disgusting spoons, awful spoons, on Miss Lynden; that's a nice thing to do, as things are at present, for a young man who is legally supposed to have come to years of discretion."

"Shut up, Tom; we're old friends, and I don't want to quarrel, but I won't hear anything against Miss Lynden."

"Who wants to say anything against Miss Lynden? She is just the nicest girl I know, and that's the only excuse for your selfishness and folly. I suppose you think you're behaving well to the girl you profess to love, by bringing her heart into her mouth every time she hears the news-man yelling out, 'Glorious victory,' to make her heart jump and her colour come and go whenever she hears the Crimean mail is in, and finally, to make her cry her eyes out because your worthless carcase has been riddled by Russian bullets."

"Well, Tom," rejoined Fleming, laughing, " it's to be devoutly hoped that you are not gifted with second-sight, because the view you are taking of my immediate future is, to put it mildly, unpleasant. Why am I more likely to be shot than you, I should like to know ? You're much more likely to run your thick head into danger than I am."

" A palpable miserable evasion of the question," returned Byng. " You're getting desperately spoony on Miss Lynden, and worse still, you are letting her know it. It's not right ; bottle your feelings up, repress your emotions as I do ; do you suppose you're the only fellow who's——" and here the speaker stopped abruptly, conscious of having in his zeal said more than he meant.

5*

"No other fellow what?" ejaculated Fleming in considerable surprise.

"Never mind, nothing, remember what I have said, drop making love to Miss Lynden," and with these words, Byng somewhat hastily left his friend's room.

I daresay Byng's advice was theoretically good, but human nature is wont to play the very deuce with theories. There is nothing like a big war to precipitate matters of this kind, and it is just when the love words ought not to be spoken that our feelings get beyond our control, and those love words slip out which are never forgotten. Ah, well, I doubt if those from whose eyes the tears are destined to flow, those who are doomed to mourn their dead, would have had it otherwise. There is something sweet in those sorrowful memories:

> " For the mark of rank in nature
>   Is capacity for pain,
>   And the anguish of the singer
>   Makes the sweetness of the strain."

CHAPTER V.

" THEY have come at last, as you always said they would," exclaimed Hugh Fleming, as he entered the Lyndens' drawing-room one gloomy day about the middle of November, " our orders for the East."

" Yes, I thought so," replied the young lady, as she shook hands, but in by no means the exultant tones with which people usually greet the fulfilment of their prophecies. Who of us have not suffered from that ever recurring, usually detestable, " I told you so." How is it that our accession to the rewards of this life are never announced beforehand, while its evils and misfortunes are so industriously foretold to us ?

Hugh Fleming should have been in high spirits at having attained his heart's desire,

but somehow he was not. He had come to
pay a farewell visit — he had had a good
many to pay, and had put saying good-bye to
the Lyndens off to the last. Good-bye, when
it is for an indefinite period, is often a painful
thing to say, even though it is mercifully
veiled from us that it is good-bye for ever.
Still no such thought oppressed Hugh's
mind on this occasion. He was off to
the Crimea, of course, everyone who wore a
sword was bound to go there now, he would
come back again in due time, a captain,
perhaps a major, who knows? But he was
quite conscious that saying farewell to Nellie
Lynden was the hardest task that had ever
fallen to his lot yet. He knew that he loved
her dearly, he knew that he ought not to tell
her so, and yet he was guiltily conscious that,
if not in words, he had been telling her so for
some weeks past, as if a genuine love story is
not told long before it is put into matter-of-
fact words. " I love you," requires no speech
to proclaim it, and put what guard we may

upon our tongues, no woman needs their assistance to learn it. After the first conventional speeches, a silence fell upon those two. It was not that, as a rule, they had not plenty to say to each other, but of late they had found the keeping up the ordinary stream of talk wearisome. Both were conscious that there was a barrier which had not been broken ; but what they had both known it must end in, had come at last. The word "good-bye" had to be spoken ; the initiative was with Hugh, and he was sore puzzled how to begin.

I once heard a well-known soldier who had won for himself countless decorations, asked in a club smoking-room what was the nastiest bit of work he had ever had. He paused a little before he answered, and it was easy to see that he was recalling the scene to his mind's eye. "Breaking to a lady," he replied at last, "that her husband had been killed at the head of the stormers that morning." Bidding good-bye to the woman he loves is the hardest thing for a soldier when ordered on active service.

"I suppose they have given you very short notice, to finish with," said Miss Lynden, woman-like, the first to relieve the awkwardness of the situation.

"Yes," rejoined Hugh; "we are all supposed to be ready to go now at a moment's notice. We embark at Liverpool the day after to-morrow. Of course, we're glad to go; but we're sorry to say good-bye to so many who've—who've been kind to us."

"We shall miss you all very much. I hear we're to be left quite forlorn for the present, as you are not to be replaced. Is that so?"

Hugh felt the situation was intolerable.

"I don't know, and I don't care," he replied passionately. "I know I oughtn't to say it, Nell—you will let me call you Nell for the last time—won't you?"

Her lips moved slightly, but she made no reply.

"I ought not to say it, Nell, I know," he continued, "but I cannot go out there without telling you I love you. I am not going to ask you to promise yourself to me, I will only ask you to think of me, and to think kindly of me. Remember, when you read any account of our doings out there— remember, there is one amongst us who can never forget you, and if ever I do anything that brings me into notice, promise to send me just one line of congratulation."

It has been before mentioned that Nell Lynden was a quiet, possessed, self-reliant young woman, but it is just these self-reliant heroines who disappoint one so cruelly at the crucial moment. If she was self-reliant she was also a warm-hearted girl, and (I apologise for her) all she did at this critical moment was to burst into a flood of tears and gasp out—"Oh, Hugh!"

For a moment Hugh Fleming was dismayed—tears usually do discompose a man— and deeply repented him of his rash avowal, but when he saw Nellie smile through her tears it gave him the courage to become practical, and passing his arm round her waist he did what was obviously his duty under the circumstances—kissed them away.

" It was very foolish of me I know, Hugh," said the girl at last, " I know you must go, but it seems bitter to part from you just now ; no doubt there are scores of women in my place, still, remember what those terrible lists are to us. Ah, it was bad enough to read them after the Alma and Inkermann, but when you are out there, my own, the very rumours of fighting will make my heart turn sick."

" Nell, Nell, this will never do, remember my darling you are a soldier's sweetheart now."

" I know," she replied, smiling, " and I am not going to be foolish any longer. But Hugh, I've hardly had time yet to get used to the position. You will let me come to Liverpool and see you off, won't you ? "

" No, I think not ; you see there is no time
to announce our engagement now, and I can't
bear to think of you in the turmoil there's
sure to be, all by yourself."

" I don't care who knows of our engagement," exclaimed the girl, proudly.

" No, Nell," replied Fleming, " but that's
just where it is, they will see you down at the
docks and won't know of it."

" Nor do I care about that, but I do care
very much about seeing the last of you."

" I can't help it," replied Hugh, " you must
be guided by me in this matter. No, Nell,
my dear, we will say our good-byes here.
There is one thing, you know, we can write to
each other by every mail."

" Ah, yes, and mind you do so. I may
keep you to myself the whole afternoon now,
may I not ? "

" Willingly," rejoined Fleming. " I am
your prisoner for the rest of the day if you
choose. I suppose I had better tell your
father ? "

" That shall be as you think best. If you don't, I must ; but Hugh, what will your own people say about it ? "

" Well, you see," he replied, " I've kept pretty straight and never given them any trouble since I joined, then, further than saying that I ought to wait till I have got higher in my profession, what can they do, except congratulate me ? Besides if, instead of the sweetest girl in England, I was about to introduce a Gorgon to the family they couldn't say anything to me just now ; why the most peccant amongst us are voted white as snow nowadays ; the most un- compromising fathers have granted plenary absolution."

" It will be a sore trouble to me if your people are very much opposed to our engage- ment," said the girl, thoughtfully.

" But you will stick to me, Nell, won't you ? " he asked anxiously.

" Yes," she replied. " I'm yours for ever ; let it be as long as it may before you come to claim me ; but I own I am nervous about what your people will think of it."

Hugh now set himself earnestly to dissipate any misgivings Miss Lynden might have upon that score. It is unnecessary to follow the conversation of the lovers further ; suffice it to say that Hugh Fleming was absent from the temporary mess which the —th had established at the "Queen's Hotel," nor did any of his brother officers set eyes on him that night.

The next day was their last in Manchester, and what time they could snatch from duty was filled by saying once more those "last good-byes," which people always feel impelled to speak when leaving their native country. Hugh, therefore, saw little of his brother officers all that day, and embarked next day hugging his secret closely to his own breast.

But there never was a man in love who did not crave to impart his madness to somebody, and few amongst us have not some friend who, though to some extent the confidant of our hopes and aspirations, is still oftener a recipient of our follies and vexations. It was so with Hugh, and by the time they had "rolled through the gut of Gibraltar," Tom Byng was fully acquainted with the story of his subaltern's love.

"Well, you've done it now," he remarked; "and all I have got to do is to offer you my hearty congratulations. Please to forget all I ever said to you on the subject; what one says to a man before he does a thing is totally inapplicable after he has done it. If this wind lasts, we shall be at Malta in no time. I wonder where they will put us up."

"From what those fellows told us at Gib., they must be pretty full there."

"Full!" exclaimed Byng. "Packed like sardines in a box, I am told; and tents in the open will most likely be our lot. Never mind; it's all on the way to the Crimea, and as for tents! why there's nothing like getting used to them while we have leisure."

Malta, indeed, was as full just then as it

could hold. Its hotels were thronged with people curious to hear the latest rumours from the seat of war—women anxious about sons and husbands. Sick and wounded officers invalided down from the front told direful tales of the difficulties of getting up provisions to the plateau still grimly held by the Allies. Both sides seemed to have stopped for breath after the furious struggle of Inkermann, and it was now rather an open question as to which were besiegers and which were besieged — whether we were investing Sebastopol, or whether the Russians had not invested the entrenched camp of the Allies. At Malta, of course, supplies were plentiful, and it really seemed almost a mockery that men were living well on that sun-baked rock, while their brethren but a little way off were near starving on the storm-swept plateau of the Chersonese. That half-dozen miles of almost trackless mire between Balaklava and the front quite explained why it was so. *Dum vivimus vivamus*, and Malta was never gayer than it was that winter. Even those most anxious to join their comrades already in front of Sebastopol were fain to confess that there was nothing doing up there at present. As far as the English were concerned, it was the same weary monotonous trench work, only relieved by an occasional sortie. With our Allies it was different. Stronger handed than ourselves, the French persistently continued to sap up to the Bastion de Mat—a proceeding to which the enemy offered fierce and jealous opposition.

Still everyone knew that nothing of any consequence could be attempted till the Spring. Whenever British regiments are gathered together, they are sure to develope three of our national particularities, they are certain to start cricket, racing, and theatricals. If it was the wrong time of year for cricket and racing, private theatricals were just the thing, and no less than two companies were organised that winter. Hugh Fleming greatly

distinguished himself in one of these, and his
Crepin, in *The Wonderful Woman*, was pronounced to have soared quite above the range
of the ordinary amateur. But though Hugh's
face flushed with pleasure at seeing himself
favourably noticed in print, yet there was
mingled with it a half-contempt that he
should be engaged in such frivolities. This
was not what he came out to do. Such
pinchbeck laurels were not the things he had
promised himself to lay at Nell Lynden's feet.
He had yet to learn that the more you can
combine relaxation with the serious business
of fighting, the better for everyone; take
your men out of themselves, let their trade
be what it will, if you want to get the maxi-
mum of work out of them. And the
successful representative of Acres will most
likely be well to the front in a hand-to-hand
mêlée not forty-eight hours afterwards.

Those were halcyon days for Hugh; nearly
every mail brought him letters from Nellie,
in which passionate love was mingled with

all the chit-chat about those he knew in
Manchester. "I hear constantly," she said
in one of her letters, "from Frances Smerdon.
What have you, or at all events some of you,
done to her? She is so bitter against you all.
I heard from her only the other day, and she
made me quite angry. 'As for the poor
—th,' she said, ' we need not fret about
them, there is always a cessation of hostilities
when they appear upon the scene. Papa
says that he thinks nothing more will take
place, and that a peace will be patched up
in the Spring. No, we needn't be anxious
about the —th; they are very nice fellows,
but they are not a *fighting* regiment, my
dear.' "

Now if this had angered Nellie Lynden, it
had stung Hugh Fleming to the quick. It
was a gibe about which all the men of the
corps were very sensitive. They were as
smart a regiment as there was in the service,
and one of the seniors of the Army List, but
there remained the bitter fact that they had

hardly the name of a battle emblazoned on
their colours.   It was luck; while some
regiments seemed always in the way when
hard fighting was going on, others, from no
fault of their own, seemed never to hand on
such occasion; the same with individuals,
though having once gained distinction, a man
can to some extent force himself forward;
yet many a young soldier has panted for the
opportunity never vouchsafed him.   The
objurgation that escaped from Hugh's lips as
he read this was anything but complimentary
to Miss Smerdon.   Although they had made
jests in Manchester, of the premature way in
which they had been *fêted*, yet there had
always been a tinge of soreness at the bottom
of their hearts, arising from this very subject,
and had anybody thought of connecting the
two, and chaffing them about it, he would
have aroused the wrath of the corps with a
vengeance.   Hugh pondered for a little as to
what could have drawn forth Miss Smerdon's
sarcasm.   Her father had been very hos-

6*

pitable to the regiment during their stay at
Newport, and she herself had been popular
with all of them. What could have made
her turn round and taunt her old friends in
this fashion?

However, Spring at last made its appearance, and despite Mr Smerdon's prophecy
brought with it neither dove nor olive-branch,
but an order for Her Majesty's —th to proceed, amongst the very first reinforcements, to
the front. The sun shone brightly as they
steamed out of Valetta Harbour. And all
signs of that dreary winter seemed to have
vanished. As Tom Byng said, "By Jove,
how those fellows before Sebastopol must
revel in this! How they must kick up their
heels after all they have gone through."

Across the bright dancing waters of the
Mediterranean the good ship rapidly makes
her way; up the Sea of Marmora, through
the Dardanelles, looking perfectly lovely in
all the glory of the early spring; has a good
passage up the usually stormy Euxine, and as

they near Balaclava a dull monotonous boom breaks upon their ears and informs them that the belligerents have woke from their winter torpor, and though as yet somewhat leisurely, are recommencing hostilities.

"Ah, Miss Smerdon will have to take back her speech, I fancy, before long," said Byng, as they threaded their way into the crowded and land-locked harbour (Hugh had read him that extract from Nellie's letter). "I wonder whether she'd feel it should she chance to see that we've been in a big fight, and that some of us had gone under in attempting to blazon the colour."

"Ah, she's been rather severe lately on our want of laurels."

"Yes, a girl who speaks of us as she does is not likely to cry much for us," said Byng sulkily.

Hugh eyed his chum queerly for a moment, and then, as he knocked the ashes out of his pipe, rejoined:

"Don't think you quite understand women

—there was a lady called Beatrice and a man called Benedick."

" Never — except in Shakespeare," said Byng.

Hugh Fleming shrugged his shoulders and walked away without reply.

CHAPTER VI.

THE TAKING OF THE QUARRIES.

"Hulloa, young un," exclaimed Tom Byng, as he thrust his head into the door of Fleming's tent, "if it was some time before we got introduced to the trenches, I'll be bound to say the big wigs are doing their best to make us quite at home in them now."

"Why, you don't mean to say we find them again to-night?"

"Indeed we do, my boy, and if you've got nothing ready to eat you'd better come and feed with me at once. I don't know yet what's in the wind, but the Brigade Major, who is an old pal of mine, told me we were likely to have a very lively night of it."

"All right, I'm your man, Tom; I shall be

ready in two minutes, and then I'll come with you."

"Yes, it's sharp practice," said Tom Byng as they sat down to dinner. "I only came out of the trenches myself this morning, but it's all fair enough. These regiments that bore the brunt of the winter are reduced almost to shadows. I met a fellow the other day whose regiment is in the left attack; he told me that they hadn't two hundred men fit for duty; so of course the turn comes heavy upon strong regiments like ourselves. That's the sherry, help yourself and pass it on. By the way, did I tell you my adventure on the Woronzoff Road this morning?"

"No, what was that?" enquired Fleming.

"Well, I don't know whether you've ever been down there. The left attack fellows generally take care of it. However, for some inscrutable reason we were told off for it last night. The trench crosses the road, and we had an advanced picket of a subaltern and thirty men, covered by a *chevaux de frise*, some eighty yards or so in advance. I'm afraid it was a bit my fault, but I was new to the post, and a trifle anxious. You see, when you're told to withdraw at daybreak, it becomes rather a nice point.

"I was warned that the Russian rifle pits commanded my trench, and would make themselves deuced unpleasant as soon as they could see. In my anxiety not to quit my post too soon I stayed a little too late. As I withdrew my advanced picket, two or three fellows had a snap at us, but no sooner did I fall in my men and leaving the main trench proceed to march them up the road, than the rifle pits at the top here in front of the right attack, commenced squibbing. To retreat leisurely may be dignified, but it's not whist. I wasn't going to lose men if I could help it, so I gave the word to double. You know that tall Irishman, Mickey Flinn?—he was doubling alongside me when he suddenly exclaimed, 'I'm shot, Captain Byng — I'm shot.'

" 'Come along, my good fellow, come
along,' I cried, as I turned round to look at
him. He was doubling as steady as any man
in the company, and gave no sign of being
wounded.

" 'I'm shot, sorr,' he reiterated, and without slackening his gait.

" 'Where, my good fellow?' I inquired, as
we still doubled side by side. 'Where, my
good fellow?—where? Come on!' I once
more cried.

" 'Right through the body, sorr,' he
rejoined, without in the least relaxing his
pace.

" 'Come on!" I cried; 'come on!' And
how the deuce a man shot through the body
succeeded in keeping up the steady double
Flinn did astonished me greatly.

" 'Yes, sorr,' he exclaimed, continuously,
'I'm shot; shot clean through.'

" Well, I continued my exhortation to keep
it up, in short, keep it up was the sum total
of my advice, and the responses to my litany

on Flinn's part were—'I'm shot, sorr!—I'm shot clean through!'

"As soon as we turned the bend in the road and were out of fire, I halted my party, that Flinn's wounds might be attended to. There was the bullet mark certainly, going straight through his great coat in front, and a hole where it had come out behind, and if ever you would have said a man had been shot through, it was Flinn.

"When we came to his tunic it was the same, but when we came to himself, there was nothing but a red mark running round his ribs. The bullet must have struck a button of his great coat in front, glanced round his body, and come out at the back. The queerest casualty I've seen since I've been at work in the trenches. The best of the joke is that Flinn's extremely disgusted because I haven't returned him wounded. It's not a bit that he wants to shirk duty, but he wants to know what's the use of being shot clean through the body if yez don't get the credit of it."

"Fall in the covering party!" interrupted the hoarse voice of the sergeant outside the tent.

"Time's up!" said Byng. "Here, Stephens," he cried to his servant, "quick, give me my revolver! It's a pity to be asked to an evening party, and not be able to take part in the fun. Now Hugh, come along!"

A few minutes more, and they were wending their way to the brigade ground where the various trench guards formed up, and were formally handed over to the colonel destined to command them.

"Who commands the —th?" exclaimed the officer in question, as he got off his horse.

"I do, sir!" replied Byng, touching his cap.

"You and your fellows are for the advance to-night, and are not likely to have a dull time of it, I promise you," said the Colonel, cheerily. "The Sappers report that those rifle pits in front of our attack are getting too troublesome to be borne with any longer ; we must have them to-night."

" You will find us all ready, sir," replied Byng, " as soon as you give the word to go."

The Colonel gave him a good-natured nod.

His own officers always said of Colonel Croker that you could be always sure when you were about to see sharp fighting. The Colonel's manner was so deuced pleasant.

There was a delay of some ten minutes or so before they moved off, waiting for the waning light to die as near away as might be ; and then under the cover of the semi-darkness the several guards moved rapidly away to their allotted positions.

Having gained the advanced parallel, Byng collected his men, and spread them in lines along the most convenient part of the parapet.

" We'll just wait another half-hour," said the Colonel, " that all may be comfortably settled in both attacks, and then the sooner we have those Quarries the better. Your men know they'll be wanted in earnest in a few minutes?"

"Yes, sir,"

"And not a shot, mind, till we've got them. We'll carry them with the bayonet. Now wait for the word."

It was a still night, and the stars twinkled brightly, although the moon was not yet up. Pulses throbbed and hearts beat quick as the little band awaited the signal, keen and anxious as greyhounds in the leash. The big guns boomed at short intervals, and there was the usual spattering rifle fire going on in the French trenches, on the extreme left. Byng and his followers stood with pricked ears, and almost breathless from excitement, waiting the word to go.

Suddenly through the night air rang out the long-expected command, "—th, Forward! Charge!"

In an instant, before the bugle could sound the repetition of the order, Byng and his brother officers had bounded over the parapet, followed by their men, and with a loud hurrah dashed across the open, straight for the coveted pits. So sudden and so un-expected was their rush that the enemy had only time to discharge a few hurried shots at their assailants. A minute or two more and Byng, Fleming, and their followers had tumbled pell-mell into the little group of rifle pits it was their object to obtain, and were engaged in a fierce hand-to-hand conflict with their tenants. A confused hurly-burly, in which oaths, bayonet thrusts, the cracking of revolvers, and an occasional death - shriek were strangely blended. It did not last long. The dash of the attack, and perhaps slight superiority of numbers, speedily told on the side of the English, and the discomfited enemy was soon seen flying back.

"Well," said Byng, complacently, as he and Fleming met at the conclusion of their little victory, "that was a very pretty scrimmage while it lasted. Well done, my lads, but don't think you won't be served with notice to quit before the night's out. This'll be a comfort to Flinn next time he is called to take a turn on the Woronzoff. I hope he's not managed to get shot through again this time."

"I'm none the worse, sorr, thank you," growled a voice from the background, "which is more than I can say for one or two of them as got in my way, but it'll take a bit more than this before the Woronzoff's pleasant for sthrolling."

"Now, Jackson, what about the casualties? Our losses are only slight, are they?" said Byng, as the colour-sergeant from the left hand company came up to make his report.

"Not very heavy, sir, as far as I can see," replied the sergeant, "but we've lost Captain Grogan."

"Grogan! Good God! killed?" said Hugh.

"Yes, sir," replied the sergeant. "A shell

burst just as we cleared the parapet, and a bit of it struck the Captain and killed him before he had led us a dozen yards."

"Poor fellow," muttered Byng; "you are senior subaltern down, Fleming. Go and take command of the other company. We're expected to hold this position till morning, remember, and by —— I mean to do it."

Hugh moved off in obedience to orders, and at this juncture Colonel Croker made his appearance.

"Well done —th," he exclaimed, cheerily. "Now Captain Byng, you've got in and you must keep in. I've got heavy reinforcements drawn up in the fourth parallel, and shall lead them on as soon as you're attacked. Attacked you're sure to be in an hour or two, only they haven't got the range as yet." And the Colonel glanced significantly at the shells flying over their heads and bursting in all directions. "The Sappers are coming up directly to reverse the parapet and connect the pits, and the noise of their parties will still more madden the Russians."

The Colonel walked quietly back to the fourth parallel, and for the next half-hour the shot and shell flew furiously over their heads, though, like the buzzing of an irritated wasp's nest, it did but little harm. On the contrary, it served to mask the noise of the now actively engaged working party. Then came a lull, an ominous lull it occurred to Hugh Fleming, as he strained his eyes through the dim starlight, seeking for any sign of the approaching enemy. He had not very long to wait. Soon he could discern a dark mass creeping along the edge of the ravine, whose object evidently was to get round his left flank before attacking it. Similarly, although Fleming was not aware of it, did Byng discover a small column of the enemy attempting to steal round his right flank. Byng had very little doubt that Hugh was equally menaced on the left. Directing his men to use their rifles, as he expected he was immediately answered from the left. Finding themselves discovered, the Russians raised their battle slogan, only to be answered by the defiant hurrahs of the English. Then ensued some twenty minutes of as stubborn fighting as it is possible to witness. True 'to his promise the Colonel had been prompt with his reinforcements, or else the —th must have been swept out of the position they had won. Twice were the Russians hurled back from their desperate assault, but their gallant leader succeeded in rallying them for even a third attempt. But the steel had been taken out of them, and they came on in a very half-hearted way to what they had done on the two previous occasions. Though victorious, the —th had been pretty roughly handled in this last struggle, and not only were many of them stretched lifeless in the trench, but the stretchers had a busy time in conveying the wounded to the rear. Among them were two of Hugh's brother subalterns, one of whom was carried off with a smashed

7*

arm, and the other a bullet through his thigh, which, when attended to, proved to disqualify him for military service for ever. The Colonel reinforced Byng's party to the extent the position would hold. Once more he impressed upon him that he must hold the position, *coûte que coûte*, and that he might thoroughly depend upon reinforcements, led by himself, to come to his assistance the minute he was seen to be attacked.

"Till the moon rises," said the chief, "you'll have a ticklish time of it, but as soon as it's light enough, the batteries will make it rather hot for the Russians, should they venture to cross that open ground."

There was little need to tell the trench sentries to keep watch that night. Little more than an hour elapsed before the enemy once more sallied forth from their lines, and made another most determined attack. If the conflict was not so long as the previous one, it was quite as obstinate, and in the course of it Colonel Croker, while personally leading the reinforcements, fell literally riddled with bullets, while another subaltern of the hard beset —th, was carried away very badly wounded. Twice more at short intervals did the Russians again return to the attack, and in the last of these a bullet stretched Tom Byng, to all appearances, lifeless on the ground, and, the struggle ended, one of the few remaining sergeants reported to Hugh Fleming that two-thirds of the men were down, and that he, Mr. Fleming, was the sole officer left of the half-dozen officers of the regiment that had marched down from camp.

Black with powder, with clothes torn to ribbons, and eyes bloodshot with the thirst to slay, they were a fierce and savage-looking band upon whom the moon now looked down. It was not likely, Fleming thought that any further attack would be made upon them, but for all that he knew he had to keep vigilant watch until relieved. He was in sole charge of the shattered remnant of the —th.   Poor Tom Byng; he never thought of his falling.   And then he thought savagely of Miss Smerdon's sarcastic speech.

"The bill," he muttered angrily, "the bill ought to satisfy her.   Five down out of six is pretty stiff.   And we have not quite done with it yet.   They will never be able to say that the —th is not a fighting regiment after this.   They must put some account of such a scrimmage as this in the papers.   It's a big thing in sorties.   I wonder whether Nell will be pleased when she reads it."   And here suddenly through the trench ran a whisper of, "Here they come again."

In his anxiety to ascertain what was doing, Hugh Fleming sprang upon the slight parapet, an act which was immediately greeted by a report of two or three rifles, the bullets of which sang past unpleasantly close to his ears.   He jumped back again into the trench, but not before he had convinced himself that so far the alarm was baseless.   Some few Russian sharp-shooters had crept along the edge of the ravine, with a view of harassing the occupants of their late position, but there were apparently no supports behind them.

The moon died gradually away before the first streaks of dawn, and no sooner was the light sufficient than the batteries on both sides engaged in a savage snarl over the disputed bone of last night. The Russians knew well that every hour their lost position remained in the hands of their assailants so much the more difficult would it be to recover. It was clear it could only be retaken by daylight at a great sacrifice. They must wait for the next night, and in the meantime, as Mr. Flinn said, "They were showing a deal of nasty temper."

It was weary work, after the prolonged excitement of the night, waiting through the early morning hours for the reliefs to come down; but they came at last, and sadly Hugh Fleming commenced to lead his worn and shattered band back to camp. It was impossible to regain the right attack without exposing the party to a certain amount of fire from the enemy's guns, and the Russians were not the men to overlook their opportunity. However, Fleming was fortunate enough to accomplish this without further casualties, and finally reached camp, where he found the remainder of the regiment anxiously awaiting their coming, and full of pride at the way they had taken and held the Quarries.

On the right, our gallant Allies had undergone similar experiences, but the splendid rush with which they had taken the Mamelon just before sunset, recalling the dash of a pack of hounds into cover, had not been sustained. Carried away by their impetuosity the victorious French chased their beaten foes to the very glacis of the Malakoff, but there they encountered the Russian reserves, and were in their turn not only hunted back to the Mamelon, but through it, and so lost the work they had so gallantly won. General Bosquet, who was in charge of the attack, was, however, not quite the man to put up with such failure as this. He hurled two brigades at once against the re-captured Mamelon, and after a brief but sanguinary struggle the French regained possession of the Lunette, though, take it all in all, at a fearful sacrifice of life.

CHAPTER VII.

MISS SMERDON'S PRIDE BREAKS DOWN.

A WELL-KNOWN novelist, who has not long since left us, ascribed the rather moderate success of one of his earlier stories to the Crimean war. It was the first time we had been engaged in a European struggle of this sort, since the invention of steam, telegraphs, and, if I may be pardoned the expression, newspaper correspondents. Then again the great battle between Russia and the Allies was practically fought out in a cock-pit, and the famous correspondent of the *Times*, then in the hey-day of his youth, was enabled to keep that paper supplied with such an accurate, I may almost say microscopic, account of the great siege as made it easy for those at home to follow it, in all its details. It might have been headed, after the manner of these times,

"The Crimea day by day." It was close upon a twelvemonth from the time the Western powers first sat down in front of the place, before the Muscovite, after gloriously half-repulsing an assault all along the line, succumbed to his assailants. Small wonder that those who were there from first to last compared it to the siege of Troy. One thing it proved conclusively, and that was that like Sebastopol, Troy was only half invested, or starvation must have compelled its capitulation long before ten years.

That several of his brother officers should gather round Hugh, on his arrival in camp, was but natural. They were all anxious to hear his account of the last night's fighting, how poor Grogan came by his death, and so on.

"No doubt you are pretty well played out, old man, but beyond that you took the Quarries with a rush, and have been fighting for them all night we know nothing; whether the wounded fellows could tell us anything

we don't know; the doctor won't allow
them to talk just yet, he is so afraid of
fever. Byng might no doubt if they'd let
him."

"Tom Byng!" ejaculated Fleming. "Why
he's dead. Shot through the head."

"Not a bit of it," exclaimed two or three
voices at once.

"Why I saw him carried away myself."

"Not a bit of it," rejoined the others. "It
was a mighty close shave, but Tom Byng is
no more dead than you are. He was stunned
and was a good bit coming to, but he has
escaped, the doctor says, by about an eighth
of an inch."

"Thank God," said Fleming. "I'm sure
I thought he was killed. How about the
others?"

"Badly wounded all three of them, still
the doctor says if he can only keep the fever
within bounds they will all pull through.
Poor Loyce must lose his arm. You're not
touched, Hugh, are you?"

"No, but I'll tell you what. I'm just froze for a drink, a wash, and a sleep."

"All right, old man, we'll bother you no more. Bustle off to your tent and we'll see nobody disturbs you. We were all turned out and kept under arms for two or three hours in case you wanted us down there," and the speaker jerked his thumb in the direction of Sebastopol.

After the excitement and fatigue of the night Fleming slept soundly for some hours. He had rapidly adopted the habits of the old campaigner, who thoroughly understands that sleep is a thing to take when you can get it. It sometimes happened that men only came out of the trenches to be marched back again before they could get their belts off, in consequence of a sudden alarm. The contending armies were like two gladiators ever keeping a keen eye for an opening, and, notably, on the side of the Russians, taking speedy advantage of it. He was awakened by a roar of laughter just outside his tent, and

hastily putting on a few things and a pair of
slippers, stepped outside and found a small
knot of his brother officers gathered round
Tom Byng, who, seated in an easy chair, with
a bandaged head, and propped up by pillows,
had apparently finished the narration of some
story which had thoroughly tickled his
audience. He silently extended his hand to
Fleming as he came forward, and as Hugh
clasped it, he said:

"Thank God! I was afraid it was all over
with you."

Byng gave a queer smile, and rejoined
with a slight motion of his head:

"Natural density saved me, old fellow.
I'm all right, but have rather an earthquaky
feeling to-day."

"What's the joke?" continued Fleming, as
he warmly pressed his friend's hand. "I
was roused from my slumbers by ribald
laughter."

"Tell him, some of you," said Byng.

"Well, it's all Mickey Flinn. Seeing Tom

outside his tent he came across to congratulate his Captain for not being kilt dead entirely, and Tom was unwise enough to chaff him.

"'Last night was worse than the Woronzoff, eh, Flinn?' said Tom.

"''Deed sorr, and it was, and it's glad I am to see your honour about again, for it's kilt dead entirely I feared you was when I put you on the stretcher.'

"'Ah, being shot through the head is worse than being shot through the body.'

"''Deed, I don't know, sorr, it's much of a muchness it sthrikes me, only you get the credit of being wounded for the wan and you don't for the other,' and with that Mickey Flinn saluted, and stalked back to his company in supreme dudgeon."

"It's all the old villain came to see me about," said Byng, still laughing at the recollection. "I believe he was glad I wasn't killed; but he's very angry because I have been returned as wounded, and he wasn't."

"Yes," laughed the adjutant, who was

one of the group; "that's a good healthy
grievance that ought to be a comfort to Flinn,
whenever the rations run short, to the end of
the campaign. He's a fine old soldier, but as we
all know you may trust the old soldier to
have his grievance."

"Yes," said Fleming, "he'll go through
any amount of hardship, hard work, and fighting ; but he must have his grievance—generally
about the veriest trifle."

And then there suddenly arose a shout
from the orderly room tent of " Mail in from
England!" followed by the sharp bugle-call
for orderly sergeants, and the group of
officers, with Fleming amongst them, rushed
off to see after their letters.

"Yes," thought Tom Byng, as he looked
after Fleming; "I counselled him not to
speak, but he has the best of it now. Letters
from home! Yes, we're all glad to get them
—ah, very glad no doubt, most of us; but
don't tell me Hugh wouldn't give up all his
letters from home, and the whole corres-

pondence of the regiment to boot, for that one letter he's expecting from Nell Lynden! I hope the young un 'll come through all safe; and after last night it does seem as if Providence was watching especially over him. I fancy he was right not to take my advice." And if one might judge from Hugh's face as he passed a few minutes later with an open letter in his hand, Byng was right in his conclusion.

Few things could have been more harassing to a romantic and imaginative young woman of those days than to discover that she had let her heart go out of her keeping before she was aware of it, to be uncertain whether her feelings were reciprocated or not, and that the man who had won her affections should sail for the East without making any avowal was hard.

Frances Smerdon was in this position, and all Nell Lynden's burst of girlish confidences about her love dream were gall and worm-wood to her friend, "Detestable gush,"

Frances Smerdon called it, and revenged herself by saying the most spiteful things of the
Regiment collectively, which were intended
to be repeated for the benefit of the one
individual who was the object of both her
love and her hate. But when, with the
Springtime, came the news that the fighting
had begun again, and also that the Regiment
had reached the Crimea, Frances Smerdon's
heart began to quail and soften. She could not
speak bitterly of men she had known well
but such a short time ago, and the finish of
whose lives she might see announced in any
morning paper. There was one man she
hated, there was one man she declared she
would never speak to again. He could not
have been blind to her love. He must have
despised it, she would never, never, never——
and then this inconsistent young lady would
burst into a flood of tears, and only wish she
could write a long letter to him.

"If he had only given me some excuse
before he left," she moaned, " but I suppose·

even if he was seriously wounded it would be an awful thing for me to write to him. As for Nell, I could box her ears, I could, for gushing to me about her love when she knows I'm so unhappy."

Now this was exactly what Miss Lynden did not know. Her own love affair had probably prevented her noticing her friend's weakness, though women seldom succeed in keeping each other in the dark on such points. Men as a rule are slow to recognise a leaning in their favour. It might be that, but, whether from policy or from a mistaken estimate of his chances, Tom Byng sailed for the East without uttering a word to Frances Smerdon that could be construed into anything more than admiration. But what did puzzle Miss Lynden much was the change that had come over her friend. It was the one girlish friendship, remember, she had ever made, and that Frances should not sympathise and rejoice with her in the flood-tide of her first love grieved the girl sorely. She

8*

so craved for a woman's sympathy in her passionate dream—for someone to talk with of her hopes, of her fears—and women had too many of those latter to battle with in love born in such troublous times.

She could not understand it—Frances seemed to have changed completely. She was witty and sarcastic about things generally; she had laughed at Nell about her "spoonishness"; told her she could not hope to keep her soldier wrapped in cotton wool when shot and shell were flying about; and that she needn't be afraid, it was a peaceful regiment, and all would be over before they got there. Angry though they made her, Nell felt that there was a hardness and bitterness in Frances' letters that had no genuine ring in it; and then, much to her amazement, Miss Smerdon's letters suddenly completely altered in tone, and her enquiries after the —th became both courteous and pressing.

As we know, whether the man she loves is

in danger, or whether he is merely passing a
lively winter in a pleasant place, make a good
deal of difference in the expression of a
woman's sentiments under Miss Smerdon's
peculiar circumstances.

The camp was rich in " shaves " that bright
spring weather. Men seemed to have shaken
off the torpidity of the winter, both mentally
and bodily, and, wondrous were the rumours
of what the French were doing, and we were
going to do, and even what the Russians
might be expected to do. Men began to
move about amongst the lines, and the half-
starved garrons of ponies, that had passed
the winter in painfully toiling with such
luxuries as their masters could lay hold of
between Balaklava and the front, waxed fat
in the ribs and sleek in the coat. Barley
was plentiful, and they no longer stood shiver-
ing at their picket pegs, with their quarters
turned to the cold blasts of the Steppes. En-
terprising sutlers erected stores on the way
to the front, and sweet champagne, dubious

brandy, and all descriptions of tinned deli-
cacies became no longer scarce, and were to
be had on comparatively reasonable terms.

A few days after the taking of the Quarries
a group of officers might have been seen
lounging on the Woronzoff road just at the
point where three or four tracks—it would
have been absurd to describe them as anything more—branched off the main road in
various directions across the Plateau, suffi-
ciently confusing, except to the initiated.
Take the one to the right for instance, and an
hour or two's easy riding would bring you
amongst the famous caves of Inkermann, and
eventuate in your certainly getting inside
Sebastopol before morning, as a prisoner.
The laughing knot of officers were of all
branches of the service, but there were a
good many of the —th among them. A fresh
regiment had arrived at Balaklava that morning and was to march up to the front that
afternoon.

Now the regiment in question was what is

termed a sister corps of the —th, which being interpreted means that the two corps had been quartered together, or as the soldiers term it, " lain together " in several places, and that the officers and men had cordially fraternised and knew each other well. The men, as a rule, showed their gratification at the meeting by being slightly the worse for liquor, late for tattoo, and exchanging forage caps, than which latter mysterious ceremony none are so significant of friendship and goodwill in the eyes of the British soldier. The officers usually celebrate their re-union by an interchange of dinners, in which they would sing the old songs, and prolong the festivities far into the night. Moreover, as it was known that the same regiment had a draft of the —th attached to it, the latter had sent their drums and fifes to meet the new-comers at this point in the road, and from thence play them into camp.

"Not much of a band you know," said Hugh Fleming, "all we can say is, it's the best we have out here. Hang it, I never properly appreciated a drum and fife before."

"Yes, you're right," exclaimed the adjutant, "a little music does brighten one up here a good deal. On my word I wouldn't despise a decent barrel organ."

"That's where the French have one pull over us," said an officer of artillery, "they've managed to bring their bands out with them. By the way, I was down in your conquest last night, Fleming."

"My conquest, indeed!" laughed Hugh, "I was uncommon glad to get out of it, that's all I know. I hope you didn't find the Russians quite so touchy about it as I did."

"No, they're quiet enough over it now; we should like to get guns into it, but the ground's so confoundedly rocky I can't see how the engineers are ever to make the sap."

"Listen," cried the adjutant, "here they come, and playing our own quick step, "Warwickshire Lads," as a greeting. Now fall in, you drums and fifes, and as soon as you catch sight of the head of the regiment strike up their own march "Hurrah for the Bonnets of Blue," and, confound you, roll it out as if you were trying to crack the fifes and burst the sheepskins."

Another minute and the head of the new regiment appeared in sight, and then the drummers and fifers of the —th crashed out their welcome to the new-comers whose own music at once ceased. Cordial hand-grips and enquiries passed amongst the officers of the two corps, for it was not two months ago since the new-comers had played the —th down the Stairs at Valetta. At this point the draft of the —th branched off to the left, in the direction of the lines of their own corps, and with them rode the adjutant and Hugh Fleming. On their arrival this batch of only just drilled recruits was at once paraded and the men told off to their respective companies.

Hugh Fleming looked carelessly on while the adjutant allotted a few to his own com-

pany. The sergeant was marching these off
when the sound of his own name made him
turn abruptly.

"Here's one recruit, sir," said the sergeant,
"says he's got a bit of a note for you."

"A note for me!" ejaculated Hugh.
"How did you get it, and what's your name,
my lad?"

"Peter Phybbs, sir," replied the boy. He
was little more than eighteen. "My sister
got it for me when she heard what regiment
I'd 'listed in, and said I was to be sure and
give it to you as soon as I had the chance."

Hugh threw one glance at the superscrip-
tion of the rather crumpled missive the recruit
had placed in his hands, and instantly recognised Nell Lynden's well-known writing. He
at once tore it open.

"Dearest Hugh," it ran, "the young
brother of Phybbs, our parlour-maid, has it
seems enlisted in your regiment. The girl's
in a sad taking about it, in which, alas, I can

only too fully sympathise with her. She seems to think, poor thing, that your powers to protect him out there are boundless, and to soothe her I write this to ask you to look after him a bit if he gets sick or in trouble. I know you will, Hugh, dear, if it's only for my sake; but I also like to think that it is another link between us ; that while his sister is watching and waiting by my side here, he is fighting by your side there. I have never seen him, but he sounds a mere boy to be sent out on such work. God bless and save you, my darling,

"Ever your own,

"NELL."

"Well, Phybbs," said Hugh. "I'm asked to look after you a bit, and you may thoroughly depend upon me as long as you deserve it. Keep straight, my lad, don't flinch from your work, and be easy with the drink, and that's all I have to say to you at present. See the old hands aren't too

hard upon him, Smithers," and with that
Hugh turned on his heel and walked off to
his tent.

"A queer letter of introduction," he said
to himself with a smile, "but I must do the
best I can for Nell's *protégée*, simply because
he is her *protégée*." He little thought those
few lines of recommendation were to prove of
more value to him ere long than any letter to
the Commander-in-Chief from the highest in
the land could be.

CHAPTER VIII.

Miss SMERDON has been making herself as unpleasant as it is possible for a vivacious
young lady to do when matters are running
askew with her, and that, needless to say,
means that Twmbarlyn House is rendered
generally uncomfortable for all therein.

"What's come to the girl?" demanded Mr.
Smerdon, petulantly, of his wife. "She used
to be the life and sunshine of the place, and
now she just mopes and snaps like a puppy
with the distemper."

"I don't know," returned Mrs. Smerdon,
anxiously; "she won't tell me, but there's
something that worries and frets her. She's
never been the same girl since her last visit
to Manchester."

The good lady did not think fit to confide

her thoughts to her husband, but she was not blinded; she strongly suspected that her daughter had brought a heartache home with her. The very servants wondered what had come to Miss Frances, and said that there really was no pleasing her.

One morning, Miss Smerdon hastily caught up the paper, as she usually did; she was feverishly anxious to see it now-a-days, though formerly the perusal of the *Times* had been either neglected or left for an idle half-hour. She was so interested, she said, in the doings of our soldiers in the Crimea. All this, though unnoticed by her father, was easy reading for a mother's eye. She could not induce the girl to give her her confidence, but Mrs. Smerdon had little doubt that Frances' heart was in a soldier's keeping. If she had thought that before, she knew it for certain that morning. No sooner had the girl torn open the paper than the head lines, " Brilliant Exploit; the Taking of the Quarries; Severe Fighting," caught her eye, and then came a glowing and graphic description of the position, of the dashing manner in which it had been carried, followed by a spirit-stirring narrative of the gallant and obstinate endeavours of the Russians to recapture it during the night, and speaking in terms of unqualified praise of the bull-dog tenacity with which the —th clung to the vantage ground they had won.

Frances' colour came and went as she read; at length she came to the postscript of all glorious bulletins.

" We regret to say that in the execution of this brilliant and successful operation Her Majesty's —th suffered severely, having no less than five out of the six officers engaged in it *hors de combat.* The subjoined list is a return of the killed and wounded on the occasion.

" Killed : — Lieut.-Colonel Croker (commanding the attack); Captain Grogan, —th Regiment.

" Wounded :—Captain Byng, —th Regiment (severely)."

The paper dropped from her hand and the blood left her cheeks. Frances turned white to her very lips, and a slight moan escaped her. Her head swam, and it was only by a supreme effort she saved herself from fainting. Her mother was by her side in an instant, while her father looked up from his letters with open-eyed astonishment, and exclaimed, " Good Heavens, what's the matter ? "

" Nothing, Matthew ; don't take any notice of her ; she will be all right directly," rejoined his wife, sharply. " She's only a little faint ; she has been out of sorts lately, you know."

" I think, mamma, I'll go and lie down ; I don't feel very well," murmured Frances, and assisted by her mother she left the room and made her way to her own bed-chamber. Arrived there, she broke fairly down, burst into tears, and sobbed like a child on her mother's breast.

Mrs. Smerdon knew that this was no time for questioning. She let the girl weep passionately on her bosom for some minutes, knowing full well that she would have all her confidence a little later. Then she loosened her dress, made her lie down on the bed, and said :

"You can't sleep, I know, Frances ; but try and lie quiet, dear, for half-an-hour. I will come back and bring you some tea then, and you shall tell me all your trouble. Who should you come to, child, in your sorrow save to the mother who bore you ? "

And before an hour was over Mrs. Smerdon knew that her daughter had given her heart away unwooed, and was tortured with shame and anguish because it was so, and that the author of all this mischief was now lying in grievous case in camp before Sebastopol.

We know that Tom Byng was in no such plight, but he had been carried away from the Quarries for dead in the first instance, and had actually figured as such in the first

returns of casualties. Luckily, the mistake was discovered in time, and " severely
wounded " was substituted for killed. Sanguine though the doctors were about his hurt
being of no great consequence, yet they were
a little chary of speaking decisively about it
for a few days, and hesitated to describe as
" slightly " a wound which might even yet
take a serious turn.

It might have been some satisfaction to
Mickey Flinn had he understood that Captain
Byng had no knowledge of how he was re-
turned in that night's casualties.

" Severely wounded ! " thought Frances,
when left to herself. Ah ! how often had
that word been the precursor of " died of his
wounds," of late. She had heard it said that
the wretched accommodation of the field
hospitals gave little chance of recovery to
those once admitted into them. Oh, if she
could but go out to nurse him ! But that was
impossible. If she could but write to him.
But no, he had never spoken—he had given

her no right to do that. And yet in her heart of hearts she believed that he loved her. Oh, she had been mad! She had been rightly punished! She had jeered at the regiment— sneered at him; and no doubt Nell had told Hugh Fleming, as she intended Nell should, and so all her bitter words had come round to his ears. How could she have been so wicked and so spiteful? How was he ever to know that such words escaped her lips in the agony of what she believed to be her rejected love.

No, she thought, she must go away. She could not stay at Twmbarlyn, for everybody, she felt sure, would read her secret in her face. She would go to the Lyndens. She hungered to hear all about the old lot, to talk of Hugh Fleming, of Tom; and her face flushed even as her lips syllabled the name. She would hear, too, what his hurt was, whether it was likely to go very hard with him — no, if Nellie would have her she would go to Manchester at once. She would

9*

write by that day's post, and then the return of her mother cut short the thread of her meditations.

As she had anticipated, Mrs. Smerdon found herself speedily taken into her daughter's confidence, and she not only soothed the girl, but proceeded, metaphorically, to bind up her wounds forthwith. The Smerdons were good, homely, as well as self-made, people, and neither of them entertained any extreme ambitions for either their sons or daughter. Smerdon had attained wealth, and with it such ascent in social status as is its inevitable accompaniment. So long as Frances married a gentleman of fair repute she was free to choose where she listed, and Mrs. Smerdon knew very well that had any of the officers from Newport, who so constantly dined with them, taken the girl's fancy, her father would have made no objection. As for Captain Byng, he had always been a great favourite with the good lady, although she had never dreamed that he had found favour in her daughter's eyes. But this may very easily be accounted for. Though Frances had always liked Captain Byng, it was not till she was staying at Manchester with the Lyndens that the liking had ripened into a serious attachment. There is love at first sight, no doubt, but it's more generally, I fancy, of a slower growth. Again, as Tom had observed, soldiers were " up in the market " just then ; and on my conscience I believe people fall in love very often for the sole reason that they ought not to do so.

Mrs. Smerdon comforted the girl very much. She made light of the difficulties of the situation. " If," she thought, " Frances has set her heart on Captain Byng, and he likes her, there is no earthly reason why she shouldn't marry him—-let him only get safely through this horrid war—and he will make her a very suitable husband." In her mother's partiality she looked upon Frances as a good match for any man. No, she saw no reason whatever why Frances shouldn't write to Captain Byng.

"You knew him very well, and there's nothing out of the way in your writing to inquire after him, having seen his mishap in the papers. Still, if you wish it, which you don't——" and the elder lady laughed merrily.

"Thanks, no, mamma; I'll write to him myself."

"Quite so," replied Mrs. Smerdon, nodding. "And now, my dear, hope for the best; it's no use thinking that just because people are ill they are never going to get over it. As for your going up to stay with Nellie, I certainly think that's advisable. Change will do you good. You will have an inexhaustible topic between you, and she will be able to give you small details about their daily lives out there, interesting to anyone, but especially to those who know—much more care for—the actors in the drama." Frances' face flushed a little at her mother's allusion to her weakness, but she had derived much consolation from her counsel and sympathy, and the thought that she saw no cause why she should not write to Captain Byng. In the course of that afternoon she despatched a letter to Miss Lynden, in which she recanted all the bitter things she had ever said about the regiment, called herself a little beast for having even thought such things, pleaded that she was very miserable, begged that she might come to her, said she had so much to say to her, and pledged herself to be on her very best behaviour during her visit. If Miss Lynden had been blind to Frances' feelings in the first instance, she could read between the lines of her present letter, thanks to Hugh Fleming. Tom Byng was a very transparent man, and, sharpened perhaps by his own experiences, Hugh had no difficulty in penetrating his friend's secret, before they had set foot in the Crimea.

When they'd got this town taken and the war finished up, he thought his friend would have no cause for despair if he asked the momentous question. Meanwhile the town took a deal of taking, and seemed quite as well supplied with provisions and munitions of war as its assailants.

Miss Lynden's answer came by return of post. Thanks to Hugh's hints she was now able to account for the fluctuations in Frances' correspondence which had so much puzzled her. She knew very well what that long talk would be about, and it was very sweet to the girl to think that at last she would have someone with whom she might talk unrestrainedly about her love.

As far as the doings in the Crimea went, no man could follow the proceedings of the Allies with closer interest than Dr. Lynden. But though aware of the engagement between Fleming and his daughter, he totally eschewed all discussion of that subject. He had some grounds for doing so ; it certainly could not be said that Hugh's family had welcomed the intelligence with effusion. To tell the truth, old Mr. Fleming was furious at the announce-ment, and only restrained from fulminating his wrath in all directions by the circum-stances of the case. "Nothing can take place at present between them but an exchange of ridiculous love-letters; Time very often dispels these illusions. Besides, if anything should happen to the boy, I should be very sorry to think that angry words had passed between us; and Master Hugh has a considerable touch of my temper about him. If he persists in his obstinacy and folly, when this affair is all over it will be quite time to let him know my mind thoroughly about such a preposterous arrangement." And then with sundry incoherent remarks, in which "young idiot," "retired doctors of unknown families," "impertinence," and strong expletives were all mixed together, Mr. Fleming senior determined to say no more on the subject at present, but to fall back on a policy much in vogue just then of "masterly inactivity."

"Oh, Nell! can you forgive me?" said
Frances, when, her journey accomplished, she
found herself once more safe in the Lyndens'
drawing-room, with her friend ministering to
her requirements in the shape of tea. "I've
said horrid things of Hugh and the dear old
regiment, I know. I could bite my tongue
out for doing so now; but I was so miserable.
I have tried so hard to forget him, but
I can't; and now he's wounded—badly
wounded—but I forgot, you don't know, and,
oh, how am I to tell you?"

"Oh, yes, my dear," replied Nell, with a
smile, "I fancy I do know—know perhaps
even more than you do, and a pretty scolding
there will be for Captain Byng next time we
meet."

"Is it very serious?" asked Frances,
eagerly. "How is he going on? Do they
think he will get over it? What does Hugh
say?"

"Hush! one question at a time," rejoined
Miss Lynden. "We must wait for the next

mail to come in. I had only one line from Hugh this time. Here it is," and the girl took the scrap of a letter from the bosom of her dress, and read as follows :

"MY DARLING NELL,—Just one line to say that I am all right; but we had a big fight last night in the trenches, and you will be sorry to hear that several of your old acquaintances were knocked over. Poor Grogan, indeed, killed. I'm so dead beat I can't write any more.

"Ever dearest, your own HUGH."

"That is all, Frances, so you see we must wait till the next mail for further tidings. I'm sure to hear again then. Hugh is very good about writing, though sometimes I get only such a scrap as this."

"It's terrible, this watching and waiting," cried Miss Smerdon. "It must be hard for you to bear; but, ah! Nell, how much happier you are than me. What wouldn't I give for just two lines like that!" and as she spoke she looked wistfully at the letter her friend held between her fingers. "Ah, if he had only given me the right to care for him."

"Listen, Frances," replied Miss Lynden, "didn't I tell you that I had something to scold Captain Byng for. If his advice had been followed I should have been exactly in your place, and Hugh would not have told his love before he left. You're a proud girl, and Captain Byng's a quixotic man, as if a man's love story ever offended a woman, even when she didn't care for him."

"Ah, my pride is all broken down now," replied Miss Smerdon, in dejected tones. "He must never know it, he would laugh at me very probably if he did. It's very disgraceful, Nell, but I do love him. You never told Hugh any of my wicked remarks, did you?"

"Well, do you know," faltered Miss Lynden, "do you know, I'm afraid I did."

"Oh, Nellie, how cruel of you. How could

you," exclaimed Miss Smerdon with flushed cheeks, starting bolt upright from the desponding attitude she had assumed in a corner of the sofa, " you know I never meant them."

" I knew they were meant more for somebody else's ears than mine," remarked the other demurely, " and I took care they got there."

" How mean of you, how wicked of you, what a wretch Tom— Captain Byng I mean —must think me ; and now he's dying——" and Miss Smerdon sobbed audibly.

" Don't be a fool, Frances," interposed Miss Lynden, a little sharply. " I quoted your tart remarks in my letters to Hugh simply because the fluctuations of your temper puzzled me. I could not understand it. It was well I did so or I should not have understood things even now. Hugh, you see, was behind the scenes the other side, and when we compared notes we came to the conclusion that Benedick had gone to the wars once

more, and that Beatrice had promised to eat
all of his killing. My dear, when next you
meet Captain Byng, I have no doubt you'll
find he has something to say to you."

"Oh, Nell, do you really think so? Do
you think he——"

"Loves you!" said Miss Lynden, laughing.
"No, I don't; but Hugh does, and that's a
good deal more to the purpose. He's wiser
than I am, and has much better opportunities
than mine of judging of Captain Byng's
feelings. *Soyez tranquille*, my dear, and wait
and hope trustfully for good tidings by the
next mail."

Oh, the humility and self-deception of a
great love! Here is quick, clever Nellie
Lynden not only saying that honest, straight-
forward Hugh Fleming is wiser than she, but
that he possesses a quicker insight into the
state of the affections! As if on this latter
point the perceptions of man are not as those
of the mole compared to the eagle with the
observations of the opposite sex.

CHAPTER IX.

POLICE CONSTABLE Richard Tarrant is somewhat disconcerted at having, as yet, failed to verify his conclusions. He had drawn a more prosaic deduction than Miss Smerdon, concerning the mysterious employment practised by Dr. Lynden in his den. When on duty, his beat often brought him within the vicinity of the doctor's house; but he spent many a sleepless night, which his obligations to the force did not impose upon him, in watching that side door of the doctor's. We know what he supposed that the rather retiring portal would open to admit; but with all his vigilance, he was fain to acknowledge that, watch as he might, he saw bodies, neither living nor dead, pass its threshold. Had he confided his suspicions to

Polly Phybbs, that young lady, after she had got over the first shock of such an accusation against the doctor, would have ridiculed the bare idea of such a thing. What the doctor might do in the laboratory she did not know, but she would have been quite certain that it could be nothing of the kind that Dick Tarrant suspected; and still more certain that if there had been the faintest grounds for thinking such a thing, nothing would ever have induced her to enter the room again. She had obeyed her cousin's command to keep her eye upon the doctor; she had always done as Dick told her, and yet even about that she had her compunctions, and only for that foolish belief she had in Dick's understanding, would have pronounced that all nonsense. That so far it had led to nothing, she was well satisfied. The doctor was a kind master, to whom she wished no harm, if, as Dick said, he was engaged in something "agen the law," well, then, she supposed he deserved to be punished, but she did not wish

hers should be the hand to bring it about.
Her young mistress too, she held in the
highest esteem, and then had she not just
written that letter to Mr. Fleming in the
Crimea? and Polly Phybbs looked upon the
ægis of Hugh Fleming's protection as going
far to ensure the safety of her boyish brother.
Still she never had refused to do Dick's bidding, and she would do it now, but it was
much satisfaction to her to find that nothing
came of it.   What had induced the doctor to
make that mysterious addition to his house?
It would have hardly attracted the curiosity
of anyone but such an addle-headed man as
Dick Tarrant.   His main idea was that
advancement in the police was easiest pro-
cured by some startling discovery of crime.
More than one had taken place since he had
been in the force, but Dick argued that he
never had any luck, let him only get a chance
and they would see what was in him.   His
superiors believed there was very little, and
were not at all likely to entrust Constable Tar-

rant with any delicate investigation. A slow thinker, one to whom ideas came but seldom, Dick clung strongly to this main belief of his, and also to that subsidiary notion that the conviction of the doctor was the case by which he was destined to achieve greatness. Now, without the slightest disparagement of the police, because it is an infirmity of human nature, there is always a disposition to make evidence chime in with conviction. Once having settled in our mind who is the author of a murder, we are more disposed to devote our powers to proving ourselves right in that conjecture than to an unbiassed investigation into who really committed it. The faculty of cool judicial analysis is rare, and it is seldom even the best detective can resist jumping to a conclusion at which he should only have arrived step by step.

That Richard Tarrant is also obstinate, it is almost needless to state. Men of this type always are. Let them once get a maggot into their head, and they cling to it with a

pertinacity that would be beyond all praise if
it were not wrongheadedness—mainly owing,
I fancy, for want of another idea to take its
place. Dick Tarrant is in this plight. He
began by suspecting Doctor Lynden of vague
offences, and must continue to do so because
he has no one else to suspect.

It is Sunday afternoon, and, in the worst
possible humour, Mr. Tarrant is lounging
about the road awaiting the advent of Miss
Phybbs. He is angry that his vigilance has
resulted in nothing so far. Mr. Tarrant is an
indolent man, and chafes mightily at nights
out of bed, which produce no compensating
result. That he should have been kept
waiting is an additional grievance; and,
moreover, he has discovered that Polly is
reluctant to carry out his orders—in fact, to
use his own expression, that she isn't half
"keeping an eye on him."

"Now," mutters Mr. Tarrant to himself, "I
ain't going to stand that, not likely you know.
Never give women their heads; that's my

10*

motto.   And if Polly thinks she's not to keep
her nose to the grindstone, she's very much
mistaken.   There's my future career all
depending upon the successful working out of
this riddle, and she thinks she ain't called on
to assist.   If she thinks after we are married
she'll have nothing to do but sit with her
hands in her lap and play at being a fine lady,
she won't do for me.   A man can't do everything himself, and my wife will have to help
keep the pot boiling."

God help poor Polly Phybbs if she should
come to wed this man, under that delusion.
He is of that sort for whom women of Polly's
class work their fingers to the bone, quite
content to keep their lords in indolence as
long as they neither ill-use nor are false to
them.

Suddenly the side door of the doctor's
house opened, that door which, watch it as he
might, he had never succeeded in seeing
used by anyone.   And out of it, to the utter
bewilderment of Constable Tarrant, stepped a

well, but quietly-dressed, lady-like woman. Although closely veiled, he felt sure that it was not Miss Lynden; he knew the latter perfectly by sight. The doctor's visitor was both taller and stouter, in short, much more of a woman, and her unexpected appearance so utterly upset his previous suspicions concerning the doctor that he neglected to do what an ordinarily intelligent officer would have done under the circumstances, to wit, follow her.

She apparently did not notice him, but walked quickly towards the busy part of the town, while Dick first stared vacantly at her, and then looked in a dazed way at the portal from which she had emerged. He was still gazing at this last, when he was startled by a voice at his elbow, saying:

"You seem rather interested in that door, my man; pray, what is it you see to admire in it?"

He turned, and to his surprise found the doctor standing by his side.

"How on earth did he come here?" was Dick's first thought, utterly oblivious of the fact that it was easy for the doctor to come out of one door while his (Tarrant's) eyes were fixed on the other.

"Nothing, sir, nothing!" he replied, confusedly. "I was only just thinking——"

"Of what?" said the doctor, suavely.

"Thinking, sir, thinking—just thinking—about nothing at all," concluded Dick, desperately, disconcerted by the keen glance with which the doctor regarded him.

"An occupation in which mankind spend a good deal of their time," said the doctor, with a slightly sarcastic smile. "I wish you a good afternoon!" and he walked leisurely away in the same direction as that taken by the lady.

"Well, I'm blowed!" remarked Mr. Tarrant, after a minute or two. "Here's a discovery? This is what comes of keeping your eye on them." And here his reflections were interrupted by the appearance of Miss Phybbs.

"Now, Polly," he exclaimed, after they had shaken hands, "you're a nice one, you are, to help an intelligent officer in the discharge of his duties. Who's that lady who visits the doctor, and he lets out of the side door? You've never said anything about her, you know."

"Lady! What lady? The only ladies that come to our house come to visit Miss Lynden, and of course, come and go at the proper door."

"Oh, oh!" said Mr. Tarrant, sarcastically; "this is what you call keeping an eye on him, is it? If you ain't got no powers of observation, you can't help it. If you can't see beyond the end of your nose, I'm sorry for you; but if you ain't altogether a beetle, it's downright wicked idleness, that's what it is."

"Oh, Dick, Dick! what have I done?" cried the girl.

"Done," replied the police-constable, in high dudgeon, "it's what you ain't done. I'm complaining of. How do you think I'm ever

going to get on in my profession if you won't
help ? "

" I assure you, Dick, I've done as you
ordered me, but I've nothing to tell you.
The doctor locks himself into the laboratory
as usual, and I haven't been called in to tidy
it up for a good three weeks. He's never had
a lady, nor any other visitor to my knowledge
all the time.   Are you sure you're not
mistaken ? "

" Mistaken ! not likely," he replied, " I
suppose you was born without gumption, and
it can't be helped, but just you attend to me."
And then Mr. Tarrant proceeded to relate
circumstantially how he had seen the lady
come out of the side door, how her departure
had been closely followed by the unexpected
appearance of the doctor at his elbow, and
how the latter had then walked off in the
same direction.

If Miss Phybbs had been a very faint-
hearted coadjutor so far, in the detective
business, yet she promised to be a very

valuable assistant in the future. She wished
no harm to the doctor and his family, but her
womanly curiosity was now thoroughly
piqued. There was a slight flavour of scandal
about Dick's story which was very titillating,
her enquiries concerning the lady's dress were
far more minute than her cousin was able to
satisfy; and if Dick recognised that his
theory of the doctor carrying on a private
school of anatomy was negatived by the
appearance of a lady on the scene, Miss
Phybbs' ready brain had already built up
another to take its place, in which, sad to say,
a very indifferent construction was put upon
her master's character ; still, in spite of Mr.
Tarrant's discovery, they were, in reality, not
one whit wiser than before. Polly had
known that men occasionally used that stair
for the purpose of visiting her master's
laboratory. She knew now that a woman
had also used it for the same purpose, and she
knew no more. Why they came or what
they came about, she and Dick were quite as

ignorant of as ever. They talked the thing over, most exhaustively, during their walk. And while Miss Phybbs ran over the list of ladies who visited the house, endeavouring to put her finger upon the one likely to be guilty of such an indiscretion as secretly visiting her master, Mr. Tarrant arraigned the doctor of every crime in the annals of the police, coining, forgery, burglary, etc., only to reject them one by one. At one time he suggested that he should at once lay what he persisted in terming his discovery before his superiors, but Miss Phybbs was decidedly opposed to that. Openly, she argued that it was useless, until they had pushed their investigations somewhat further, and arrived at something more definite. Inwardly, she believed herself upon the track of a domestic scandal, which, though eager to get to the bottom of, she had no wish should go beyond the family circle. And, moreover, would turn out a case with which the police had no concern, so when they eventually parted, it was agreed between them that their lips should be sealed for the present.

The next day Constable Tarrant's duties called him to the head quarters of the police in the city, and while there, lounging about waiting for orders, he heard some of his superiors discussing a communication that they had received from Scotland Yard, relative to a considerable quantity of base coin, with which the Metropolis had suddenly been flooded, and of the fabrication of which they had so far failed to find the slightest clue. They described the coin as beautifully manufactured and all evidently the work of the same hands. "The constructors are past masters of their craft and must be provided with very superior plant and machinery. There are probably two or three employed in the minting of it, but the issuing must comprehend a very extensive organisation. We need scarcely add, to lay hold of the principals is of the greatest possible importance."

" I don't believe we have anyone here on
the smashing lay.   At all events not such
artists as these are described to be.   We may
have one or two of the inferior ones about,
but they would be in a very small way of
business."

" No," rejoined one of his brother officers,
thoughtfully, " I don't think such a lot as
they speak of could be here without our knowing it. Not likely but what they'd try to
pass some of the stuff in a big place like this.
What little bad money we've come across
lately is of a very inferior manufacture, not
calculated to deceive anybody who looked at
it twice."

Richard Tarrant sucked all this in greedily.
He had settled in his own mind that Dr.
Lynden was offending against the laws, and
that if Dr. Lynden was not so doing in one
way he was in another was a fact fixed and
incontrovertible in Dick Tarrant's head ; if
he was not carrying on that illegal school of
anatomy then doubtless he was manu-

facturing bad silver by the bushel, and upon
no other grounds than these did he once more
decide in his own mind what was Dr.
Lynden's secret occupation. But though
both he and Polly kept watchful eyes upon
the side door it was without result. It was a
subject of much regret to Miss Phybbs that
she had not been a little more punctual in
keeping her appointment that afternoon, as
she would then probably have caught a
glimpse of that lady, and veiled though she
might have been, Miss Phybbs confidently
asserted that she would have known her
again anywhere; but to recognise her from
Dick's description was, she ruefully admitted,
impossible. Yes, there is no doubt a
pronounced taste in dress offers great facili-
ties for identification. The famous Lord
Brougham is said to have been constant to
shepherd's plaid—a material scarce known
to us in the present day—for his nether
garments. There are men in London
whose hats we could swear to, and con-

fidently predict their presence in the house as we pass their head-gear on the hall table; and I can call to mind a well-known lady, whose taste for bright colours was so conspicuous in her raiment that people at Lord's and Hurlingham made appointments to meet in her vicinity, as a rendezvous, that, though movable, could be seen from afar. If only this unknown lady had but had a penchant of that description. As it was, neither Tarrant nor Polly Phybbs saw any probability of coming across the mysterious stranger unless she should again pay the Doctor a visit.

But there is something in luck, and busy one morning in the heart of the city on some mission of Miss Lynden's, Polly could hardly withhold a cry of exultation upon catching sight of her master talking earnestly with a well-dressed woman who she had no doubt was the lady she was so anxious to catch sight of. She easily contrived to pass them, not too closely, but near enough to obtain a good view of the latter's face. It was one she had never seen before.

" She may visit the master by the side-door," sniffed Miss Phybbs, " but she's never come in at the front "; and her suspicions as to the respectability of the unknown became stronger than ever.

She turned back and repassed them, still contriving to keep unnoticed herself, which was all the more easy from the slow pace at which they were walking and the earnestness of their conversation. And Polly felt then that there was no fear of her not recognising the stranger in future.

A tall, well-preserved woman of forty, on a rather large scale ; with an indolent grace in her movement that would have made her a striking figure in any drawing-room. She was richly but quietly dressed, and that she saw her now for the first time Miss Phybbs was certain, though she and the Doctor were apparently old acquaintances. Polly had neither time nor inclination to follow them, but remained satisfied with having succeeded in identifying the stranger. She determined on her way home to say nothing of her morning's adventure to Dick, believing that if she only got to the bottom of it, it would turn out to be a petty scandal, which was no concern of the police.

CHAPTER X.

MRS. SEACOLE'S.

" It's eight o'clock, and the Crimean mail's in, and please, miss, Miss Nellie said I was to tell you that all's well," exclaimed Polly volubly, as she drew back the curtains and threw up the blind of Miss Smerdon's room one bright May morning.

" The mail in!" cried Frances, as she bounded out of bed, plunged into her dressing-gown, and dashed off to Nell's room, to pick up such crumbs of comfort as that young sybarite might choose to drop from the snug depths of her couch, and perhaps at twenty, when thoroughly in earnest, to lie in bed and read love-letters is as entrancing an occupation as a maiden need hope for.

" Captain Byng is all safe," said Miss

Lynden, " the return was all a mistake.
Hugh says he had the closest possible shave
of being killed, and they thought at first he
was so ; he was stunned with a bullet, but is
really only very slightly wounded, and doing
well."

" Thank God," said Frances.   " I almost
wish now I hadn't written to him."

" Oh, Frances, Frances!" rejoined Miss
Lynden, laughing, " you're a little the oldest,
and I used to think a good deal the wisest,
but oh, my dear, you're a sad goose.   Here
you are in love with a man, and believe in
your heart that he's in love with you, and
just because he hadn't got the pluck to speak
up before he left England, you regret that
you've written him a very proper letter, to
enquire after him on seeing that he was
severely wounded.   A very proper letter I
dare swear it was — I shouldn't wonder if
it began ' Miss Smerdon presents her com-
pliments to Captain Byng, and begs to enquire——' "

" Stop, oh stop, you tease ; it wasn't a proper letter, and that's the reason."

" Oh, never mind the reason. I know all about that. I ought to be shocked, but I'm only very glad you were a sensible girl."

" Now tell me what Hugh says, at least as much as may reach the public ear."

" Thank Heaven he's safe ; tiresome boy, he says so little about that terrible night, and I do feel so proud of him. His letter's full of nothing but dog hunting, divisional races and all that sort of thing. I'm sure, to read it, the Crimea seems to be a most lovely climate, and they're all having the greatest possible fun out there. It's hard to realise from his letter that they are actually fighting, and that men are being killed day and night. But now run away. I must really get up and dress. I will read you all the gossip of my letter at breakfast ; at present I've hardly read it myself."

Frances Smerdon walked off to her own room echoing her friend's reflections.

11*

"Yes," she murmured, "that's just what the best of them do; when the work is serious, they make light of it, and also of any grief that may come to them. There was poor Algie Barnard, at Cowbridge, last year, they said he threw the steeplechase away by his bad riding; he made no reply but fainted in the weighing-room, and then they found he had broken two ribs, and that the muscles of his right arm had been laid open in a fall he'd got on the far side of the course. Tom makes light of it, but I've very little doubt his wound is serious." And then Miss Smerdon proceeded to dress, and rack her memory in the meantime for every record in which injuries to the head had terminated fatally; and as her experiences in that way were principally connected with the hunting-field, by the time she had remembered two concussions of the brain, one case of paralysis, and another of permanent affection of the spine, she had brought herself to a very low and contrite spirit with which to join the breakfast table. Could she but have seen the object of her solicitude in the course of that day, I think she would have almost grieved to think so much womanly pity had been wasted upon him.

If a Crimean winter can be as hard and disagreeable as an English one—and with the exception of one particular, in the matter of fogs, it can quite match it — the country rejoices in one glorious superiority as regards climate. Winter does not linger there all through the spring and half-way through the summer as it does in England, but once got done with, it breaks into genuine spring ; not such a conglomeration of wet and bitter east winds as usually signalises the advent of that season with us, but bright skies, balmy breezes, and all the delights that the poets sing of — and which we so rarely witness. It cannot be said that many flowers came with the spring in '55, for everything that would burn had been burnt by the army during that pitiless winter, and the poor flowers had been so ruthlessly trampled in the mire that the few which had survived had a hard struggle to get their heads above the ground.

However, with the sunshine, as aforesaid, came great exhilaration throughout the camp ; copious supplies of all sorts, and such a multiplication of stores, canteens, cafés, restaurants, etc., as to look as if the Allies would be permanent colonists, with no intention of ever returning to their native countries, to which the establishment of a railway from Balaklava to the front still further contributed. About half-way between these two points on the main road, a large wooden building, half-store, half-restaurant, had been opened by a middle-aged coloured lady, who had somehow or other obtained considerable popularity amongst military men in the West Indies. What she had done out there I don't know, but Mrs. Seacole soon became a familiar name to the Crimean army. Horse and Foot, Hussars and Artillery, Naval officers and Newspaper correspondents, all.

drank and dined at Mrs. Seacole's. It was a sort of high change for gossip and stories. Men from all parts brought the news of the camp thither, as a common mart for the exchange of all such commodities. Many dinners came off in the snug room at the back of the front saloon, which was the general lounge ; matter of no little diplomacy at times, these dinners, as, unless previously ordered, the procuring of a table was impossible.

Perched upon a barrel in the saloon, with a short pipe in his mouth, and bearing no sign whatever of having been severely wounded, sat Tom Byng, indulging in gayest badinage with an old friend who was chaffing him about his late narrow escape.

"It won't do, Tom," said the Hussar ; "you must be ruled out of it by all the conditions of war. You were carried away for dead, and we really can't have you coming to life again in this way. Just think of the confusion it would make out here if other people behaved as you have done! Why, we should never know where we were, or who commanded anything. Now I'm very sorry for you, but in justice to the regiment——"

"Shut up, Lockwood," cried Byng. "Just ask how long it's going to be before that dinner's ready; I'll show you then whether I am alive or not."

"But you're not, my good fellow; in justice to the regiment you can't be. I don't want to counsel extreme or immoral measures. There is no reason for your completing what the Russian so clumsily attempted; but you must surely see that it is your duty to withdraw yourself from the army as quietly as may be, and so allow the step to go in the regiment. Consider, my dear fellow, you were killed!"

"No more of your chaff!" rejoined Tom Byng. "Let's have a sherry and bitters. I don't think any of our fellows would care to get their step at my expense."

"No, old man," returned the other, as

they made their way to the counter, " I'm
sure they wouldn't. And nobody can be
more pleased than myself that that Russian
miscalculated the thickness of your head."

And now a gentleman in his shirt-sleeves,
called by courtesy a waiter, announced to
Lockwood, the presiding genius of the feast,
that dinner was ready ; and the *convives*, some
half-dozen in number, trooped into the back
room to do it justice.

" Are you going to run that big bay horse
of yours, Fleming, for the Division Cup next
week ? If they don't make the hurdles too
stiff he ought to have a great chance," said
Lockwood, the keen edge of their appetites
being somewhat appeased.

" Yes," replied Hugh, " he's improved a
good deal in his jumping of late."

" Well, he need to," remarked an officer of
the Rifles. " I was over the course yesterday,
and they've got a stone wall in it that will
take some doing I can tell you. It's a good
four foot and a half high, and no give about

it. A real proper crumpler for those who happen to hit it hard."

"Well," rejoined Hugh, laughing, "I shall find out if the 'Bantam' can jump anyhow."

"For your sake it's to be devoutly hoped he can," said the Rifleman. "However, the Meeting will be great fun, and we want something to wake us up a bit, this d—d trench work is getting monotonous. 'Pon my word I haven't heard a joke or a good story for the last week."

"Right you are," said Byng, gravely. "The whole thing is getting slow, deuced slow. If it wasn't for Mickey Flinn I'd have forgotten how to laugh."

"And who's Mickey Flinn?" enquired Lockwood.

"A distinguished ornament of my company," said Byng, "with a very poor opinion of those who guide and direct him. We were down in the trenches the other night, and amongst the men was a young recruit only just out from England. Whether the poor fellow was a little flustered, it being his first time under fire, or whether, as he said, he had strayed a little from his party and lost his way, I don't know, but Mr. Flinn took it into his sagacious head that the boy was trying to desert. Well, he got hold of a young non-commissioned officer and they made the boy a prisoner. And then came the formulating a charge against him. They could not bring him up for deserting, because he obviously had not deserted, they had only caught him straying towards the town, so they finally charged him before the Colonel with 'attempting to enter Sebastopol without leave.' The Chief burst out laughing when he heard the charge, and exclaimed, ' Why, confound it, that's what we've all been doing ever since we came here.'"

" And what did Mr. Flinn say?" enquired Lockwood.

" Oh, he was heard discoursing to his comrades the whole afternoon on the subject, saying, ' It's without lave, mind you, makes the difference.' He is evidently firmly imbued that, 'If they'd only permission he and a few of his pals would be inside Sebastopol in no time.'"

"I know the sort," said the Hussar, "there's no end to that fellow's jaw, but he'll fight as long as he'll jaw and ask for no better diversion. But you're wrong about the siege; you fellows that half live in the trenches can't see it, but to men like myself who only have a look round occasionally, it's palpable how close we're creeping in. It cannot be long now, at all events, before you have a shy at the town."

Lockwood was right in his prognostication, but what he did not dream of was that the desperate assault, when delivered, should result in failure, and that in less than three hours both French and English would have been driven back, and nothing left them but to bury their dead — nearly three months more destined to elapse before the famous siege was brought to an end.

However, the dinner came to an end, the bill was paid, and horses and ponies called for, and then swinging themselves into the saddle the majority of the party rode off in the bright moonlight, across the plateau, to their respective lines. Before reaching their own camp, Byng and Hugh Fleming had bidden good night to their companions. Hugh's servant rose from a seat outside his master's tent as they approached, and, as he took the pony from him, said:

"The mail's in from England, sir. I've put your letters in your tent."

"Good night," said Byng, as he also dismounted, and strode away to his own dwelling, envying Hugh the letter he knew he would surely find awaiting him, and feeling utterly indifferent towards his own correspondence. Yet he was fond of his own people too, but he had no need to feel anxious about them; and like most men in those days, hardly realised the uneasiness and nervous solicitude of the women at home—

mothers and sisters filled with considerably more anxiety for sons and brothers than they deserved.

There were three letters on the table, the superscriptions of two of which were quite familiar to him ; but the third was in an unknown hand, and that unmistakeably a feminine one. Tom gazed at it curiously, with an indistinct idea that he had seen the hand before, although he could not recognise it. He opened it, and then sat down on his bed to read it by the light of his solitary candle.

" DEAR CAPTAIN BYNG," it ran, " We are dreadfully concerned to see by the papers that you are dangerously wounded. It is terrible to think that those we have known and " [here the word " loved " had been palpably erased] " and liked should be in such constant peril. You can't think how I feel for poor Nellie Lynden—it must be so awful for her to think that her lover is in the midst of all these dreadful scenes. I am sure

she must shudder every time she opens a
paper for fear of coming across Hugh
Fleming's name in it."

("Hum!" muttered Byng, savagely. "Con-
sidering the pleasant things she has said about
Hugh and the rest of us, I suppose she's disappointed to find that we're in the thick of it
at last.")

"I have been staying with her, and she
bears up beautifully. And now, dear Captain
Byng, you must find time to write a line
about yourself. We only know what the
papers tell us, and that is that you are dangerously hurt, and that's quite bad enough
news for your friends and relations, for all
those who really care for you. We shall all
be so very anxious to hear how you are going
on. I shall never believe that you are in a
fair way to recovery till I get a line from
yourself. Let it be ever such a scrap, I shall
feel miserable, that is, mamma and I will feel
miserable, until we learn from your own hand
that you are getting well again. With much

love and sympathy from us both, and hoping to hear from you soon, believe me, dear Captain Byng,

" Ever sincerely yours,

" FRANCES SMERDON."

There is a slang phrase in the present day that so exactly describes the effect that letter had on Tom Byng, that I cannot refrain from using it. It made him " sit up." The letter fell from his hand as he finished it, and he started bolt - upright from his crouching attitude, and wondered what it all meant. Surely a girl could hardly write a letter like that to a man she disliked. It was very odd, and after thinking it over for some minutes Tom felt so utterly bewildered at this unexpected epistle that he felt it necessary to fill a pipe and smoke and muse over it.

He read the letter over three or four times, and finally came to the conclusion that the ways of women were past all understanding, and that he must see if he could pump Hugh

Fleming on the subject a bit to-morrow. Poor Tom, if he had been making a match three miles across country, the chances are he'd have contrived to get seven pounds the best of it; nor was he likely to throw away a point of odds on the race-course, nor trump his partner's thirteenth at the whist table, but when it came to the opposite sex he was but as wax in their hands. One of those men, who, though not particularly impressionable, find it so difficult to say " no " to a woman's request. Frances Smerdon had nobody to blame but herself for the present state of affairs between them. Despite his quixotic resolutions she could have made him speak " an' she had listed " before he sailed, and she knew it.

CHAPTER XI.

In his bewilderment over night, Tom Byng
had forgotten to glance at the order book
which was lying on his table, otherwise he
would have found that his recreations for the
next day were amply provided for him; that
he was detailed for a court-martial in the
morning, and that in the evening he was once
more for the trenches. The consequence
was that he found no opportunity for that
insidious cross-examination of Hugh Fleming,
and it so happened that Hugh, who since the
death of Grogan had been acting as a
captain, was not included in the covering
party formed by the —th in the evening.
On his arrival at the brigade ground, Byng
found he was for the advanced trenches, and
though in those weary watches that had

gone by, a man had oft-times much leisure
to brood over his affairs, yet the nights had
waxed much livelier of late, and those in
the advance had to be so continually on the
alert, that they had not much time to meditate
on a love chase gone awry, or how to assuage
the angry importunities of creditors whose
patience was at length exhausted, two circumstances that a year ago claimed a good deal
of attention from most of them.   Although
nothing but the occasional monotonous roar
of the big guns broke through the quietness
of the night, yet Tom and his comrades kept
vigilant watch and ward.   They were dealing
with an enemy bold and energetic, who
threw no chances away, and whose skirmishers
stole up nightly as near as they dared, to see
if too fatal a sense of security might grant
them the opportunity for a sortie which they
were always seeking.   However, daybreak
came without even an alarm, and the sun
shone brightly out over the shattered town,
heralding the advent of a glorious day

12*

towards the very end of May. Byng was
sitting with his back to the parapet of the
trench, musing dreamily over Frances Smerdon's letter and what reply he should make
to it, when he was once more recalled to a
sense of sublunary matters by his more mer-
curial subaltern, who suddenly exclaimed :

"I say, Tom, do you remember what day
this is ?"

"Yes, Wednesday," replied Byng, lazily.

"Wednesday ; yes, sir ; *the* Wednesday, by
Jove ! it's the Derby Day, and what a day
they've got for it.   Do you recollect going
up last year and seeing Andover win ? "

"Yes," laughed the other ; "and how we
all backed King Tom, and saw our horse run
a good second on three legs ; showing that
but for the mishap he ought to have won."

"Ah, yes, but what fun we had all the
same.   What a lunch we had with those
dragoon fellows over on the hill.   They were
all on Andover—drank buckets of champagne
to celebrate his success, and insisted upon

our drowning our losses in the same manner. Ah, we were a credit to the regiment on that occasion!—patterns of sobriety to the whole British Army!—after having been engaged in such a revel."

" *Tempora mutantur,* as they taught us at school," laughed Byng. " Last year pigeon pie, plovers' eggs, and Geisler's brût were hardly good enough for us, and now I'm dying for the sight of that villainous servant of mine with the tea and cold bacon. Surely they're awfully late with our breakfast."

" No, just eight," rejoined his companion, glancing at his watch. " Listen, there go the clocks inside," and he jerked his head in the direction of the town.

A few minutes more and two or three servants belonging to the regiment made their appearance, carrying their masters' breakfasts with them. Very much to the astonishment of Tom and his companions came also a French officer, in the uniform of the Zouaves, the triple row of gold lace

round his *kepi*, and the elaborate embroidery
on the sleeve of his smart, dark blue jacket,
indicating that he was a captain, just as much
as his shaven forehead, *farouche* manner and
voluminous red *pantalons* added "and of the
Zouaves."

Tom raised his cap politely to the French-
man, whose *kepi* was off instantly in return,
and then could not help casting a look of
enquiry at his henchman.

"The Colonel commanding the third parallel, sir, told me to bring this French officer
to you. And will you be so good as to show
him all there is to be seen in the advance."

The French officer with a flourish of his
cap commenced a voluble speech in his own
language, to the effect that if he might tres-
pass upon the amiability of Monsieur he
would wish to see what we were doing in
the Front. Tom's knowledge of the French
language, like that of the majority of his
brethren in the English army, was limited in
the extreme, and the quick-witted Zouave

saw at once that he was not understood.
He changed instantly into the Anglo-Saxon
vernacular.

"Ah, monsieur," he continued, "you no
like to speak French. You English all can,
but you nevare will, *mon ami*. I am engaged
like yourself, in this stupide siege, knocking
our heads for months against this pig of a
town. I sometimes wish I was back in
Africa ; chasing the Kabyles was more amus-
ing than this. This morning I said to myself
—' *Mon cher*, you ennui yourself, you get the
rust, you get the—what do you call it—ah,
bored, you require the change, you want dis-
traction.' I said to my chief—' *Mon colonel,*
this fatigues me, these pigs of Russians will
not knock me on the head, although, *ma
foi,'*" he continued, with a shrug of his
shoulders and a grimace, "' they have been
making it lively enough for us lately. With
your permission to-day, I will go and look at
our gallant Allies. I will study the little
lanes and ditches they make, and see if I like

them better than our own.' And now, Monsieur, I must throw myself upon your good nature, as soon as you have finished your breakfast. Permit me to offer you a cigarette," and having handed his case to Tom, the Zouave selected one for himself, and throwing himself on the ground, proceeded to smoke and chat as easily as if he had known his companions all his life. He was very communicative about his past, he gave them to understand that he was a Parisian by birth, and that Paris was the only place fit to live in. 'But you do not live there for nothing, my friends ; and when one has come to the end of one's resources, there is nothing for a gentleman but the Seine, or Africa and the Zouaves. I chose the latter, and *parole d'honneur* I have never regretted it. It's a wild service ours, but it makes the pulses tingle in your veins—there is not one of us but what has won his rank at the sword's point."

Tom felt there was something fascinating about his guest, in spite of his somewhat braggadocio manner. He had the bearing, moreover, of a man who had certainly been accustomed to good society, and Tom knew that what he said of his corps was true, and that the dare-devil troops of which he was a captain had little reverence for any officers who had not won their grade under their own eyes. Breakfast over, Tom began his task as *cicerone*, and was much struck by the shrewd, soldierly criticisms of the stranger.

" Ah, yes," he said at length, " that flank battery of our friends opposite it is which enfilades the *boyau*, which I came up between this and the third parallel; but, *mon ami*, what do you propose to do next? Your engineers must know that you can go no farther; the ground is too hard. This is your advanced trench of all, I presume? " And as he spoke the French officer leaned his elbows on the parapet lazily; "and to say nothing of the *abattis*, you're a long way from the Redan." He continued to stare at the great earthwork in question, alongside Tom, although more than one bullet whistled past their heads. Suddenly he sprang upon the parapet, and, not to be outdone in hardihood, Tom immediately followed his example.

"*Sacré!*" said the Zouave, laughing; "*mais*, your company is undesirable. They will think we are the leaders of a storming party." And even as he spoke, the persistent attentions of the Russian sharp-shooters once more sang past their heads. "*Peste!*" he continued, throwing away his cigarette, and making a comical grimace at Byng. "This is getting a little too hot to remain. Adieu, monsieur." And in another second he had bounded down the far side of the parapet, and was flying as fast as his feet would carry him in the direction of the Redan, waving a white handkerchief, which he had hastily drawn from his pocket, as he did so.

For an instant Tom was taken aback, and then the truth flashed upon him that he had unwittingly been entertaining a Russian spy,

and had shown him all round our advanced
position. He never hesitated for a moment,
but at once started in hot pursuit. Either he
must bring back his treacherous guest a prisoner, or he would be well-nigh chaffed out
of the army, when the story of his entertaining that *soi-disant* Zouave got abroad. Tom
could run a bit, and it soon became apparent
it would be a very fine thing, in spite of the
lead he had stolen, for the Russian to hold
his own. It was impossible for either side to
fire, the chances being about as much in
favour of hitting one man as the other. The
parapets on both sides were thronged with
men who had jumped up from the trenches
to see this impromptu match, and though
Tom had gained very little upon him, yet,
the spy had this point against him—Between
him and the great Redan ran the *abattis*, and
though, from the straightness of his path, the
spot where he could slip through was doubtless
all prepared for him, yet a slight delay was
inevitable, and it was a fine point whether

he could pass that before Tom's hand was upon him. Nearer and nearer they came to the barrier, and it was soon evident to all the spectators that Byng was the better "stayer" of the two, and a ringing cheer from the British trenches recognised the fact. A hasty glance or two over his shoulder, speedily convinced the fugitive of the same. He saw his pursuer rapidly closing on him, and suddenly pausing for a moment in his flight, he drew a revolver from his breast and deliberately fired at his foe. He only precipitated events, for blown by his run, and with a hand that had lost its accustomed steadiness in consequence of his exertions, he missed his man, and before he could repeat the shot a tremendous blow from Tom's fist stretched him well-nigh senseless close under the *abattis*.

A roar of exultation arose from the spectators on the one side, and a yell of disappointment from those on the other. The two men were still in such close propinquity

that it would have been perfectly impossible
for the riflemen on either side to interfere,
even had there not seemed to be a tacit
understanding that the struggle between the
two men should be regarded in the light of a
duel, with which the onlookers had no right
to meddle. For two or three minutes the
men remained at the foot of the *abattis*, the
Russian recumbent and Tom leaning over
him, with the pistol now transferred to his
own hand pointed at his enemy's head.

"I'm going to either take you straight
back as soon as you've recovered your wind,"
said Tom, in the quiet, steady tones of a man
who is greatly in earnest about what he says,
"or scatter your brains out here and have
done with it."

"Bah," rejoined the other, with a fierce
flash of defiance in his grey eyes, "I have
played and lost. I know the penalty, as well
here as at the back of your trench an hour
hence; quick, Monsieur."

"On the faith of an English officer your

life shall be spared if you render yourself a prisoner. Refuse," and Byng once more pointed the pistol at his opponent's head.

"*Sapristi*," rejoined the Russian, as he rose to his feet, "I've not much choice, but while there is life there's another chance, and you guarantee me that?"

"I'll pledge my word for your life," returned Byng, still keeping a firm grip of his prisoner's collar.

"The game was worth it," rejoined the Russian, as he walked towards the English trenches, in the grip of his captor. "A majority against a file of musketeers and a short shrift; now I suppose it means a prison for an indefinite period. *Fortune de la guerre.*"

"It's not likely that we shall let you go to make use of the intelligence you've collected," replied Tom, as he handed his prisoner over the parapet into the hands of his own men, who, though regarding him with the contempt that employment as a spy always brings upon the detected, still could not withhold a tribute of admiration to the splendid audacity with which the Russian had played his part.

Tom marched his prisoner to the second parallel, and there handed him over to the Colonel commanding in the trenches, and told his story, concluding with :

"I have pledged my word for his life, and I must be allowed, sir, to make good my promise."

" You may rest quite easy on that point, Captain Byng," returned his superior. " I will relieve you of your charge, and shall send him direct to head-quarters with that intimation."

The *soi-disant* Zouave had listened with the utmost nonchalance to the story of his misdeeds, but as Byng turned to leave, he exclaimed :

" Adieu, monsieur. May I ask the name of the officer to whom I am indebted for my life ? "

"Captain Byng of the —th," replied Tom, shortly.

"Captain Byng—how do you spell him? B I—no, B Y N G. I shall recollect that name. Byng, you have saved my life, and some day, perhaps, who knows? it will be my turn. It's a queer world," and with a shrug of his shoulders Lieut. Ivanhoff raised his *kepi* to Tom, and started with his escort on his tramp to head-quarters.

For the next few days Tom Byng's adventure with the Russian spy was the talk of the camp; and that the story as it was bandied from mouth to mouth should meet with much embellishment, was but natural. There were scoffers who declared that the whole thing was a friendly running match, got up to relieve the tediousness of the advanced trenches, that a deal of money had changed hands in the transaction, that the Russians had paid in paper roubles which were unnegotiable in our lines; in short, the story was bruited about with whatever garnish crossed the imagination of the jesters of the army, and in a week incidents in the Crimea were so narrated that the chief actors failed to recognise them.   There was a well-known officer who, when wounded, was reported by the papers to have exhorted his fellow sufferers to bear their agony patiently, but camp gossip gave a very different version of the pithy speech which he made on that occasion.   As for Lieut. Ivanhoff, he remained interned on the banks of the Bosphorus until the close of the war, and years afterwards obtained high distinction in that campaign in which the intervention of Europe compelled Russia to stay her victorious career, and sign peace under the very walls of Constantinople.

CHAPTER XII.

THERE is a very fairly sized crowd gathered on the plateau before Sebastopol; half the officers not on duty have drawn together to see the fourth Divisional races decided. But for a few flags one would have hardly recognised that a day's fun of this sort was proposed, and that the race card (there are cards, gentlemen) shows no less than five events, not including the "moke race," to be decided. No Crimean race meeting could be brought to a satisfac· tory conclusion without this latter institution, and there is a Light Dragoon who is the very *bête noir* of all owners of likely mules, and who well nigh sweeps the board (I had well nigh said of cups) of purses for this interesting race.

There is an absence of stands, tents, and a

good many other adjuncts of an ordinary
race-course, notably the total absence of ladies,
which gives a business air to the whole thing
which is utterly fictitious.   In reality there
is no end of gossip and laughter over the
whole affair, and although the races are all
correctly printed on the card there is little
attempt at keeping Newmarket time here.
We start comfortably when everyone is ready,
nor are there any very close restrictions about
colours; breeches and boots most of the
jockeys have managed, but the racing jacket
is not strictly *de rigeur*, although from the
number of them that crop up it seems that
a good many men must have been impressed
with the idea that it was a useful thing to slip
into the bottom of a bullock trunk.   There is
much quiet lunching going on—not such as
you see at Epsom or at the back of the stand
at Ascot, but "just a snack, and a glass of
phiz, you know," yet partaken of amidst as
much mirth and good fellowship as ever it was
at the above-mentioned meetings at home

13*

The great event of the day is the Divisional
Open Cup, for which there are only four
competitors, but those four are supposed to
be the best representatives that the Army can
boast, though they might not, perhaps, prove
of much account amongst a lot of Selling
Platers at Newmarket. These things, you see,
are comparative, we all know the proverb of
the one-eyed man, and the present quartet re-
present the Kings of the Crimean turf.
About the merits of the four there is much
difference of opinion—that the Bantam and
Thunder are the pick of the basket is generally
conceded; which is the best is a matter of
contention. In turf parlance they can both
race and stay, but whether they are safe
jumpers is a little open to question. The
second Divisional Open Cup is a steeplechase
—that is, the best imitation that three miles
over artificial fences can compass.

Handy Andy's party, who are very sweet
upon their horse, begin picking up all the
long odds they can obtain, they swear that

their horse doesn't know how to fall, and that what he may lack in speed will be more than compensated for by his superb jumping powers. As for the owner of the fourth, he fairly admits he's afraid the company is a little too good for him, but says that he likes a ride, that his horse is very well and a safe jumper, that he shall just trust to the chapter of accidents, and that he shall at all events have a good view of the race. That the —th should be deeply interested in the Cup is not surprising. Is not the Bantam the property of one of their own officers? And is not Hugh Fleming going to ride it himself? There is a certain *esprit de corps* in these things, and from the Colonel's tenner to the drummer's shilling, the regiment are on to a man. There is much discussion about the stone wall, about which the owner of Handy Andy and his friends are especially jubilant.

" Tear an ages," cries the former, a Major of the Connaught Rangers, " av' it was only a foot higher I'd come in alone. There's not one of the lot such a lepper as my horse. Why I'd lay a level fifty I'd ride him in and out of the pound at Ballinasloe."

A little way off Hugh Fleming is in earnest conversation with Byng. He is carefully listening to his mentor's final instructions before weighing out.

" You see," says Tom, " nicely as the Bantam jumps, still he's young at the business, and it's quite on the cards he may make a mistake if he's flurried. We know he can jump the stone wall, and that's the ugliest fence on the course, because we've been schooling him over one just like it for the last three weeks. Take a good pull at him when it comes, and let him have it easy. The only horse you can't afford to let get away from you in the race is Thunder, and I fancy he'll no more want to hurry at the stone wall than you will. As for the other two you've so much the heels of them you can catch them any time. Whether we can beat Thunder we don't quite know, but anyhow

I don't think you'll find you've much in hand."

Needless to say there is no ring, and such wagering as there is is done amongst the spectators themselves. More than one holder of Her Majesty's commission tries his 'prentice hand at book-making and gets bitten with a madness destined to cost him dear in days to come. A little buzz of criticism runs through the crowd as the competitors for the Cup take their preliminary canter. "Thunder looks very fit." "Who will lay me three to one to a tenner about the Bantam?" "What the deuce does Tom Joskins mean by running that old crock of his?" "He's a good horse, I'll take fifty to five about his chance." "Good horse if you like, but he's got into rather too good company this time." "You can put it down," and a babel of similar remarks are bandied about as—the preliminary over—the four competitors make their way to the starting post. Being the race of the day, and numbering so few runners, their jockeys have contrived to appear in correct costume. The flag falls without delay, and at once the rider of Handy Andy takes the horse to the front, and in the words of his owner—" Begins pounding away in real earnest." The horse certainly is a magnificent jumper, but he can go only one pace, and his jockey is quite aware of it. He knows that his chance of victory must depend upon Thunder and Bantam either falling, or from their riders, in fear of such casualty, suffering him to obtain so long a lead that they are unable to catch him, but the artilleryman who is riding Thunder is cunning of fence, and was well-known between the flags before the war broke out. He is not the least afraid of his making a mistake at present, but he does know that a tired horse is very apt to blunder, and thinks that he would rather have a little in hand and be able to take that wall easy in the second round, for they have to traverse the course twice.

Handy Andy meanwhile sails gaily along in

advance, with Thunder lying at his quarters; the black jacket of Hugh Fleming some two lengths in arrear, and Tom Joskins on his old crock whipping in.

And now came one of those curious incidents which when seen on a race-course always remind one of the way the coloured bits of glass fall apart on the turning of a kaleidoscope. As they came to the wall, the young Irishman who was riding Handy Andy, thinking his horse was accustomed to it, sent him at the jump with a wild whoop and a flourish of his whip. The result was disastrous; for, swerving from the whip, Handy Andy jumped just across Thunder, and the two came down together in a confused heap. Hugh Fleming, in order to keep clear of the collision, pulled his horse so sharply to one side that the Bantam had to jump the wall almost sideways; the consequence was, he struck the wall slightly, blundered upon landing, and after struggling gallantly to recover himself pitched forward on his knees and head and rolled over, leaving Tom Joskins, who had got safely over to the right, alone in his glory.

At such an unexpected collapse of the race, quite a shout went up from the spectators, and numbers of them galloped off as hard as they could to the scene of the accident. Hugh Fleming and the Bantam soon struggled to their feet again, but the riders of the other two horses lay where they had fallen; and a whisper ran round the hillock, which served the purpose of a grand stand, that both men were killed. Whether this was the case or not, it was quite certain that neither made any attempt to rise, which usually betokens serious disaster.

Tom Joskins, wide awake to such a chance as had befallen him, wasted no time in looking at what were the results of the collision, but took his old horse by the head and sent him along best pace, quite aware that the further he got on his journey before any of his antagonists got up, the better. He went on for

some time before he even ventured to throw
a glance over his shoulders, and then found
that there was nothing anywhere near him.
He thought he had it all to himself, so commenced to take it a little more easily ; and it
was not until he passed the hillock and heard
the warning cry of his friends, that he became
aware there was anything left in the race but
himself.

Hugh had never lost hold of the bridle, but
both he and the Bantam were rather shaken
by the fall; and even when he had regained
his saddle and set his horse going again,
Hugh felt that he must give him a little time
to recover, and that any attempt to hurry
him at present would prove fatal. He wondered in his own mind whether it was of any
use persevering when he looked at the tremendous lead that Joskins had got of him.
His horse might be the quicker of the two, but
then he dared not make use of his speed just
yet, and in any case was it possible to make
up all that ground before the race was over ?

"No matter," muttered Hugh, "I'll see him over the stone wall a second time at all events. It settled three of us the first round, it might settle him the second."

But it was not to be. Joskins' old crock jumped the fatal wall without the slightest mistake, and though the Bantam ran game as gold and materially lessened the gap between him and his leader, yet he never could get fairly within hail of him, and Hugh, when he found pursuit was useless, pulled up and left Joskins to secure an easy victory.

"Well, after such a turn up as that," exclaimed the owner of Handy Andy, "it's to be hoped the Engineers have something for us to-night. If there's anything they want taking they'll find the Rangers in a lovely humour for it; they are broke to a man."

"I'm afraid," rejoined Byng, "our fellows are in much the same state; by-the-way, what do the doctors say of the two victims of the accident?"

"Knocked about a bit and shook," replied the Major, " but they are not broken seriously. Poor Tim Donovan, the theatrical young beggar, he rode as if he was showing off a horse at Bartlemy Fair." The further events of the day have nothing to do with this history; that moke-racing Hussar once more carried off the race of those quadrupeds, in his usual artistic fashion, sitting well back on the animal's quarters, in his shirt sleeves, and with his gold-laced forage cap set jauntily on one side.

Tom Byng, over a solitary pipe in his own tent that evening, reflected rather ruefully that Miss Smerdon's letter was still unanswered. Circumstances had prevented him from conferring with Hugh Fleming in the first place ; and secondly, Hugh, out of sheer *malice prepense*, had not only declined to be pumped, but, worse still, could not be induced to talk the thing over ; whenever Byng brought the thing fairly forward, Hugh either changed the subject, or at once turned the subject round to his own love affair, and that once started, he had so much to say that his auditor was more likely to grow weary than to get a word in. Still, that letter had to be written, two mails had already gone out, and in mere ordinary courtesy he could no longer delay sending a reply. Through Nellie Lynden, Frances would of course be aware that his injuries offered no excuse for his silence. What was he to say? He loved this girl, but he could not forget that she had laughed at him, and flouted the Regiment. Few people like to be laughed at, and ridicule has made more bitter enemies than ever good sound abuse has done. There are men who would sooner lead the forlorn hope than be the laugh of the town for three days, and the woman who forgives a man for placing her in a ridiculous situation shows a magnanimity scarce to be counted on. Pens, ink, and paper lay before him, and still this man, who had never hesitated an instant to risk his life for the capture of a spy, could not make up his mind to write a few lines in reply to a pretty girl's kind enquiries after his health.

"Here goes," he said at last—"she's laughed at me once, she shall have no opportunity to laugh at me again, as, if I allowed an atom of sentiment to appear, she certainly would."

"DEAR MISS SMERDON," he wrote—"Very many thanks to you and Mrs. Smerdon for your kind enquiries. You have, of course, heard by this that my being returned wounded was a mistake, and I can assure you than I never was in better health and spirits that I am just now. If the work out here is a bit hard at times, there is at all events plenty to eat and drink—two very important things when campaigning—and we have undergone none of the bitter experiences of those who were here the first winter. Although not wrapped in 'cotton-wool,' and taking our share of the hard knocks, we are as a whole

doing wondrous well. With kindest regards
to yourself and all at Twmbarlym,

"Yours sincerely,

"THOMAS BYNG.

"Camp before Sebastopol, July 30."

When Miss Smerdon received this terse
reply to her letter she flushed to the roots of
her hair, ground her little white teeth, and
cried with very shame and vexation. She
had never felt so humiliated in her life. She
—as proud a girl as ever stepped—in the
madness of her passion, had stooped to tell a
man she loved him! Who could put any
other construction upon such a letter as she
had penned? How she wished she had never
written! How she wished her letter had
been as icily cold as Nellie had laughingly
suggested. What must he think of her?
Ah, he had his revenge now! Here were
her own bitter jibes thrown contemptuously
in her face. She pictured him with almost a
derisive smile on his lips as he posted those

curt few lines in reply to her own too effusive
epistle.

Shame on her! She had told her secret
again and again in that wretched note! No
man on reading it could doubt that the writer
proffered him her love—and at that thought
Frances buried her face in her hands—
unasked. What had she done? Forgot her
very sex, offered herself as a wife and been
rejected. It would have been better for her,
she thought, if that Russian bullet had gone a
trifle lower, and then she could have wept
openly over his death, and have been spared
this nethermost misery. Ah, no, Heaven
help her, she did not mean that; God watch
over and save him, and send him safe through
the perils that surrounded him, although he
never could be anything to her now.

It comes hard upon a woman to have the
precious spikenard of her first love rejected,
and Frances Smerdon's had gathered in
strength from the very efforts she had made
to repress it.

She said no word to Nellie of the letter she had received. It had been brought up to her room early in the morning, and therefore Miss Lynden had no positive knowledge on the subject, but she soon saw in the girl's face that she had heard from Byng, and from her making no allusion to her letter, had no doubt that it was unsatisfactory. Frances seemed as interested as ever, when the conversation turned upon the Crimea, but Nellie noticed that instead of taking her share in it, as she had done heretofore, she was now content to be for the most part a listener. As for Tom Byng, I don't think he was quite so well satisfied with that composition of his, as he was when he first posted it. At all events Hugh Fleming heard no more of Miss Smerdon from his chum, and marvelled much what he had said in reply to that young lady's enquiries.

CHAPTER XIII.

ALTHOUGH Dr. Lynden had been a comparatively short time in Manchester, he had achieved a considerable social status there amongst the better and more refined circles. A suave, courteous gentleman who had evidently seen much of the world, and could talk well on most of the leading topics of the day. His knowledge of foreign politics was regarded with profound respect by his intimates. His forecasts of the strange events of that stormy period had proved wonderfully correct, and what Lynden thought of things was a question constantly asked by the leading business men there to whom the war was excessively repugnant. Some few objected to it on moral grounds, and still fewer on the conviction that the game was

14*

not worth the candle ; that the struggle was unnecessary ; that we were pulling the chestnuts out of the fire to serve the French, and that Russia would willingly have undertaken to do nothing that would interfere with our interests if we would only have kept out of the quarrel ; but to the bulk of the Manchester men the war was distasteful, as it always is to men who get their living by trade. The extension of business is not brought about by the winning of battles. War must of necessity be paid for by the nations indulging in it, and has never yet conduced to the acquisition of riches, which is, after all, the main object of all manufacturing industries, or for the matter of that of most other employments in this world.

In the very beginning of the trouble the Doctor had prophesied that it would all end in war. When people pooh-poohed him and said it was ridiculous to suppose that we should ever take part in another European war—that in these days of advanced civilisation it was preposterous to think that we should have resort to such a barbarous way of adjusting our differences, the Doctor replied :

"It's just that belief that you will never engage in another European war that will bring it about. That is Russia's idea also. As for civilisation—it exercises very little restraint on the passions when roused. Human nature never changes, and asserts itself in defiance of civilisation whenever you come to the crucial test. Your rulers think you will not fight ; but the nation is on the boil, and will have it so. Yes, there will be war, and not a little one, you will see."

Not only had the Doctor's prognostications proved correct upon that occasion, but either his foreknowledge or his information about the march of events was singularly accurate. He took the keenest interest in the struggle in front of Sebastopol. He had carefully studied the best maps it was possible for him to procure; while his knowledge of our

numbers in the Crimea, of what reinforcements we had under orders to join the army
in the field, and of what our garrisons in the
Mediterranean consisted, was remarkable.
Not only was he a close reader of the daily
papers, but it was pretty certain that information concerning the war reached him from
other quarters. He was always willing to
discuss the situation in the Crimea with Miss
Smerdon and his daughter.

" Ah, yes," he said one afternoon when he
came in for his cup of tea, " the drama pro-
gresses apace. With the fall of Sebastopol
will end the first act. That we should take
that, is necessary to our insular pride ; and,
even if we wished it, it is hardly likely that
the Russians would allow us to re-embark.
The French, I see, have taken the Mamelon—
do you know what that means? That is pre-
paratory on the part of our Allies to a
request that we will take the great Redan,
which, it is said, they find a thorn in their
sides. Yes, it is probable that the curtain

will fall on the first act before the end of the month. And then, ah, then—what next? We shall have dealt Russia a blow at the extremity of her empire, but we cannot get at the heart. Napoleon tried that—and a pretty mess he made of it. We have no Napoleons now."

Dr. Lynden had usually been singularly accurate in his prognostications concerning the siege, and he was so far right that a general assault on the place was imminent, but what never occurred to him, any more than it did to many of the chiefs actually present before Sebastopol, was that the attack might fail. The siege had already lasted seven months, and it was not to be supposed when the Allies did deliver an assault it could be anything but a *coup de grâce*. Why, even in this affair of the Mamelon, the Zouaves had reached the ditch of the Malakoff, and it was believed, had they been properly supported, they could have taken that work. Oh no, the first act must be very nearly played."

" You think," asked his daughter, " that the final assault will take place before June is over ?"

" Yes," replied the Doctor. " The trenches are a perpetual drain upon our army, that can be endured but little longer, while the Russians have left thousands by the way side on that terrible march across the Steppes, but when men, as in their case, believe their ruler to be both their king and their God, they'll be always ready to die for him.

Miss Smerdon's first impulse on the receipt of Byng's letter, had been at once to return home, but when she found that Nellie abstained from questioning her on the subject she reflected that her mother would be scarce likely to show such reticence, and so came to the conclusion that she had best stay where she was for the present. The Crimean war exercised a great influence over people's minds at that period, and to a romantic girl like Frances, with a special interest in the welfare of one of the actors in the drama, it became a positive fascination. She heard, somewhat more quickly, to say nothing of more directly, through Nellie, of what was taking place there; and then at Twmbarlym, there would be nobody to explain the intention of the siege operations so lucidly as the Doctor. Even Polly Phybbs had at times her scrap of information to give concerning it derived from letters received from her brother, and there was no piece of intelligence from the —th but what was worth listening to, in the opinion of the two girls.

There is nothing like a common bond of hopes and fears, to draw people of different grades together. Miss Smerdon's heart at that time yearned towards anyone who had near and dear belongings in the Crimea. This caused her to unbend somewhat towards Polly Phybbs, and once more her thoughts travelled in the direction of Blue Beard's chamber. True, she was mainly absorbed in the war, but for all that her mind at times would wander to other things. Again she

talked the subject over with Polly, and found
that young woman now quite as curious as
herself about it.   But Phybbs, while carefully
listening to all Miss Smerdon's views of the
mystery, avoided any mention of her own
suspicions.   Still the result of their joint
curiosity was that, while Frances was perpetually teasing the Doctor to be allowed a sight
of the laboratory, Phybbs was constantly
hovering about its door, prepared to take
instant advantage of finding it open.   The
Doctor was much too keen an observer not to
become speedily aware of this, he further was
not long in discovering that a rather bullet-
headed young policeman was also taking un-
wonted interest in the side door of his house,
keeping his eye on it, indeed, in such clumsy
fashion as caused Dr. Lynden to give way to
a fit of low, silent laughter.

   " Oh, dear," he muttered, " these provincial
police don't seem to have acquired the very
elements of their profession or they never
could have set such a young numskull as that

to keep watch over *me*. I wonder what it is they suspect me of. It does not much matter, they have guessed wide of the mark, I have little doubt. That girl Phybbs too is always lurking about the door of the laboratory; well, she would make nothing of it if she got inside; it would take an agent of the French secret police to do that, and even he might come, and welcome, give me but a few hours' notice of his visit. True, I have done it before successfully, but I don't like living under surveillance. Phybbs, my good girl, you are an excellent servant, and I don't mean to part with you. My charming Miss Smerdon, too I really must calm the fever in her blood. There is only one way to cure women of an attack of curiosity—gratify it. Ah, I will leave the secret portal open to-morrow and give you both the desired opportunity, and you will find nothing! Now this pudding-headed young policeman—the idea of watching my house must assuredly have been put into his head; he never would have conceived it of his own intelligence. Hum! I should rather like to know what crochet it is that his superiors have got into their brains."

True to his resolve, the Doctor next morning, after lounging into the drawing-room and announcing that he was going into the city, departed, leaving the door of the laboratory ajar—a circumstance speedily noted by Miss Phybbs. That young woman jumped at the chance, and determined to institute a thorough good search through the apartment, and see if she could lay her hands upon any slight feminine belongings, such as ladies do at times leave behind them—a glove, a handkerchief; she might even discover a note, letters, or something of that sort; also at the same time if there was anything to indicate the correctness of Dick's suspicions—that worthy having of late endeavoured to teach her what was the principal plant of a coiner's trade, as far as his somewhat imperfect knowledge on the subject extended. Bells might have rung that morning, but they would have rung unheeded, as far as Polly went, until she had finished her inquisition, but after giving an hour's harder work to her search than she had ever bestowed on the dusting of the room, she was fain to confess herself beaten. There was not the slightest vestige of anything that could convict the Doctor of receiving female visitors, or indulging in the manufacture of base silver.

" There is no proof of anything whatsomever. There is nothing but nasty jars and bad smelling bottles. Anyway my notion is better than Dick's. We do know a lady came out of that door—which is more than can be said about a bad half-crown."

Phybbs took care to let Miss Smerdon know that the forbidden chamber was open, and Frances could not resist taking a peep. A few minutes satisfied her. She was in search of nothing, and her idle curiosity was speedily gratified. Jars, bottles, and crucibles were only to be rendered interesting by the Doctor being there to explain what he did with them.   Frances indeed was disappointed at not finding drawings of cabalistic figures, a skull or two, a stuffed alligator, a glass mask, and all the usual paraphernalia with which the workshops of the alchemist or astrologer were garnished, according to the old plays and romances.

Dr. Lynden, as an ordinary chemist, was a very commonplace person, but in those higher walks in which Miss Smerdon pictured him, he was to be regarded with profound respect and veneration.   The Doctor's prescience with regard to events in the Crimea had lately induced Miss Smerdon to playfully express her belief that he was an astrologer, and that his prophecies were simply the reading of the stars.

" But," as she said to herself, " there was no telescope, and as for skulls, why, there wasn't even a skull cap."

She felt no further desire to enquire into the mystery of Blue Beard's chamber, unless by the special invitation of the Doctor himself.

It was not likely that anything would have come from Constable Tarrant's self-imposed task if he had not been helped by the chapter of accidents. Dick was not at all the man calculated to shine as one of the sleuthhounds of the law. He lacked not only the keen powers of observation, but the untiring watchfulness necessary for a detective. He was a rather stupid, indolent young man, whose idea of hard work was to superintend other people doing it, and especially did he prefer that the said hard work should conduce more or less to his benefit. He would speedily have wearied of keeping bootless watch and ward over that side door, but for one thing, notwithstanding his compact with Phybbs, Mr. Tarrant had communicated his suspicions to his superiors. They had listened to him half-disdainfully, for they had no faith whatever in his intelligence, but the senior of the two or three officers to whom his tale was told, had almost derisively complimented him, and ordered him to persevere in his vigilance.

"There might be something in it," said Evans, one of the sharpest officers of the force, when Constable Tarrant had retired. "I don't suppose there is, it's hardly likely that a man like Doctor Lynden, moving in the best of society in the place, should be running an illicit mint. Still," he continued with a grin, "we know the benefits of education and improved machinery. Your tip-toppers don't live in garrets and slums now-a-days, but on first floors, and dress like swells. Now this gang are real clever, you'll admit that; Scotland Yard, you see, is clean beat about them, and say the mintage is inimitable."

His comrades nodded assent, listening evidently with much respect to Sergeant Evans' words.

"All this points to it's being the work of tip-toppers. Now it's a curious thing that a man should take a house here, and build out a laboratory with a private stair communicating with the street. They say he's very clever, and all that; but his experiments in chemistry must be for his own amusement. Now there's one grain of truth in what Tarrant says, " What does he want with a private door all to himself? "

" Just so," said Inspector Fumard, approvingly.

" If these smashers," continued the Sergeant, " are in Manchester, we must look for them in the least likely places. I'll see if I can make anything out of Dr. Lynden."

If the Doctor has anything to conceal, it will be well for him to take heed. Constable Tarrant he might laugh at, but it is a cat of a very different colour which is now watching the mouse-hole.

That Sergeant Evans should take to either lounging about or walking up and down like a sentry outside the Doctor's door was very unlikely ; but before a week was out he had acquired some information about him which, though it puzzled the Sergeant, convinced him that the Doctor had certainly mysterious avocations. Evans' high position in the Man-

chester police enabled him to make enquiries
which would have been impossible for anyone
not so situated. He discovered for one
thing, that the Doctor, besides carrying on an
extensive correspondence, was in the habit of
sending numerous cablegrams to Odessa.
This of itself struck him as singular in a gentleman not engaged in trade. What might
be the contents of those cablegrams the companies would not have told him if they could,
but they did let him know that they were all
couched in cypher, and how this could bear
upon coining, the Sergeant was entirely at a
loss to conceive.

Another discovery he made which was quite
compatible with the Doctor being engaged in
that illicit pursuit was, that a remarkably
lady-like woman was in the habit of strolling
from the railway station in the heart of the
city out to the suburb wherein the Doctor
lived, that though she apparently never noticed
the house, she never turned until she had
passed it, and that her constant appearance had

not attracted the attention of Police-constable
Tarrant could be due only to his crass stu-
pidity. Another circumstance which speedily
struck the astute Sergeant Evans, was how
singularly capricious this lady was in the rose
she wore in her bonnet. She dressed so
quietly that nothing but a trained eye would
have detected this slight but constant varia-
tion in her head gear. The rose was sometimes red, sometimes yellow, sometimes white,
but to Evans it was speedily as clear as noon
day, that these were perfectly understood
signals to the Doctor. Whenever the rose
was red, so surely, as soon as the lady had
strolled out of sight, did the Doctor emerge
from his house, and follow in the direction
she had taken, that the pair met, walked and
talked together the Sergeant easily ascer-
tained, and that their interview invariably
ended at the railway station from which the
lady returned to town. On the occasions
when the rose was of another colour he found
that she usually returned from her walk to

15*

Manchester and the Doctor made no attempt to follow her. Sergeant Evans was puzzled, but this much did seem clear to him, that the Doctor was in close correspondence with some individual or individuals in town, which correspondence was deemed too important to be entrusted to the post; that the gang of coiners they were so anxious to pounce upon were artists of the first calibre there was no doubt, but what was the object of this lady-like woman travelling perpetually up and down from London to Manchester merely to exchange a few words with the Doctor either in the streets or at the railway station? Had she carried back parcel or package with her, he could have understood that she was the medium by which the base coin manufactured by the Doctor was transmitted to his associates in town, but she carried nothing with her but a hand bag, and into that he had contrived to obtain a peep which convinced him that it contained nothing in that way.

The Sergeant, in his own vernacular, was fairly " flummoxed."

CHAPTER XIV.

THE eighteenth of June had passed and gone with a result that astonished the Allied army pretty nearly as much as it did Dr. Lynden. After the Quarries and the Mamelon nobody doubted but that when the assault did take place we should get in; and that it would take place very shortly was evident. That it would be a pretty tough piece of work it was quite clear. We might not perhaps get possession of the whole place in the first instance, only succeed, perhaps, in capturing the great Redan and the Malakoff; still, that we should be fairly beaten all along the line, and with nothing to show for the terrible loss of life incurred in the assault, except the cemetery taken by Eyre's Brigade, would have been

credited by no one; the cemetery, too, as
the men of the left attack contemptuously
remarked, they could have taken any night
with two companies.

When the news was first flashed beneath
the waters to England, you may judge the
terror it struck to the heart of Nell Lynden
and her friend. Those first head-lines in the
papers spoke only of a general assault on
Sebastopol. "Terrible Repulse; Frightful
Losses." Bitter lines to women who had
those near and dear to them in the Chersonese.
Dr. Lynden was always perfectly willing to
talk over the successive events of the war
with the two girls, but that his daughter had
any personal interest in news from the
Crimea he had persistently ignored. He had
never alluded to her engagement—seemed,
indeed, to regard it as a passing fancy which
separation had effectually put an end to, and
Nell was quite aware that in the event of the
worst she would have to bear her sorrow by
herself, that she need expect no sympathy

from him. Though fond of his daughter, the
Doctor was a hard and proud man, with an
iron will under his suave and courteous
manner, and he deeply resented the extreme
coldness with which Hugh's relations had
taken the announcement of the engagement.
As for Frances Smerdon, he had no idea
that she had any pecular interest in the march
of events. But the terrible list came at last,
without any mention of the —th, and when
the full accounts, and also a letter from Hugh
came to hand, it turned out that the Regiment had been held in reserve, and not engaged at all that day.

"It is very singular," remarked the Doctor,
"it upsets all calculation, the first act is not
over so soon as I anticipated. Well, they are
like cocks in a pit—bound to fight it out—
they cannot run away. I am not clear
that it is not the best thing that could
happen to us. If the Allies did but know it,
this tremendous struggle at the extremity of
her empire is the most exhausting thing for

Russia possible. And when Sebastopol does fall—what next? Ah, then—if Russia could only obtain some compensating success elsewhere—take Paris, for instance, peace might be possible. After swopping queens, Miss Smerdon, one may offer to draw the game."

The siege dragged on. There was no particular action, but incessant skirmishes, and the list of trench casualties grew perfectly portentous. It was like a running sore on both sides, and cruelly weakening to the two antagonists. The lines of the Allies drew closer and closer round their foe, and it was evident to the keen observer that the Western Powers and the Muscovite must once more speedily close in the death grip. And with the early days of September came the fourth bombardment, which preceded the fall of the famous fortress.

*　　　*　　　*　　　*　　　*

It had been rather a sore subject in the —th that Hugh Fleming had met with no reward for the taking of the Quarries. He had brought the victorious but shattered band back to camp, and the regiment, though proud of the " Well done, —th! " with which their Brigadier had ridden up and congratulated them the next day, were still alike hurt that no honours had been vouched to them in recognition of this their first deed of daring in the Crimea. Poor Grogan's step had been filled up by the senior subaltern, who happened not to be present in the trenches on that occasion. But that Byng should have had a brevet-majority, and that a company should have been found for Hugh Fleming, the corps was unanimously of opinion. If there was not one vacant in the regiment, there could be no difficulty in finding such a thing just now ; every probability, indeed, of there being considerable promotion to bestow very shortly, as it was pretty generally understood that the assault would take place in the next day or two.

The regiment is for the trenches this night, and Byng and Hugh Fleming are standing in front of the former's tent, watching the storm of shot and shell that is raining down upon the doomed city, and to which the Muscovite still replies sullenly and fiercely, if not quite so vigorously as he did three days ago.

"We shall hear for certain when we get to the brigade grounds," said Byng, "but I should fancy it will come off to-night. This *feu d'enfer* can't go on much longer, we haven't the ammunition for it, we've silenced some of their guns, but it will be a toughish job all the same."

"Yes," replied Fleming, "they are no flinchers, and not likely to give in without hard fighting. Here comes the Adjutant, about to tell you off to some peculiarly delicate piece of work, shouldn't wonder."

"I've just run across, Hugh," said the official in question, "to shake hands and congratulate you on your company, although I'm sorry to say we are going to lose you."

"Lose him!" said Byng. "What on earth do you mean?"

"I've just had a note from a chum of mine, Kenyon, he's on the Head-quarter staff you know, and he tells me that the Quarry Gazette has come, and that Hugh here is transferred to a Lieutenancy and Captaincy in the Grenadier Guards. You've got your brevet, old man, there are no general orders to-night. They are too busy, I suppose, down at Head-quarters, but you'll both be gazetted to-morrow."

"We mean business to-night then?" said Hugh.

"Assault to-morrow, all along the line," replied the Adjutant. Three rockets from the French rings up the curtain. "Once more, congratulations on your promotion, though, as I said before, we shall all be very sorry to lose you."

"Well, I shall have one last turn with the old regiment, anyhow," said Hugh.

"Yes, and a pretty lively one too," said the Adjutant, laughing, "for, from what the brigade-major told me, we are to be in the

thick of the fun from the very beginning.
However, as far as that goes, I fancy there
will be very few left out of the game before
it's finished. Ah, there goes the fall in," and
all three officers hurried off to the parade-
ground in answer to the shrill note of the
bugle. " Well," said Tom, as they walked up
and down, " I wonder how you will get on in
the Guards? Out here, their life is pretty
much the same as ours, but your promotion
will most likely take you home, and then you
will find soldiering in London very different
from soldiering in garrison towns and country
quarters."

" But I don't want to go home," said Húgh.
" There's a battalion of the Grenadiers out
here ; I suppose I can join that ? Why should
I be sent home ? "

" Because there's a lot of fellows in England
dying to come out here ; because you've had
your chance, and are bound to give some of
the others theirs, because you are the junior
of your rank, and, like other juniors, must

expect to do the dirty work, drill recruits, lick stout young labourers into soldiers, etc."

"By Jove, I never thought of that," rejoined Hugh. "This promotion isn't half as good a thing as I thought it. I'd rather hang on, and get a company in my own regiment."

"Nonsense!" said Byng, laughing. "Pay, promotion, and plunder, are the three things that they say a soldier should never pass when they come in his way. But here comes the chief, fall in."

A few minutes more, and the —th found themselves part of a long, dark column, which was winding like a serpent on its way to the trenches. The heavy roar of the artillery was incessant. Shells whistled and spluttered through the soft summer night, the air seemed alive with meteors, and every now and then a heavy thud, followed by an angry explosion that burst close to the winding column, and the sudden stumbling of two or three men, proved the messenger of death had been launched only too successfully. The advanced trenches were gradually crammed with men, and bitterly did the chiefs of the reserves deplore the lack of one or more sheltered *places d'armes* wherein they might bestow their men. That the Russians, after all these months of practice, should have got the range of pretty well every part of our lines it is easy to imagine, but fortunately the pitching a shell from a distance with accuracy into a ditch, which is what a trench virtually is, is a task that tries the powers of the most expert Artilleryman. But where the trench expanded into a battery, it was very different. There the Muscovite had a bigger target to aim at, and the men who served the guns suffered terribly during the concluding months of the siege. All through the night roared the thunderous cannonade on both sides, the air hissed and hurtled with the savage missiles, while in the crowded trenches pulses beat high, and men strained their eyes in search of the first grey streaks which should herald the coming day.

" Daylight," said Byng, pointing to the sky.

" Now for it," muttered many an anxious lip, and with ears erect men awaited the sharp word of command from their chiefs, and the shrill call of a bugle. Neither came, and slowly the word ran through the trenches that there would be no assault until the Artillery-men had had some hours' pounding at the Russian lines. Our foes had taught our leaders a lesson, and shown that much as our guns might knock their defences about in the daytime, their power of restoring those de-fences by night was almost magical. If the fire raged furiously all night, it was a very storm of shot and shell, now that the sun was up, and the gunners on each side had a fair sight of their opponent's batteries. The sun was high in the heavens, yet still went on the constant roar and crash of cannon and mortar, and still no signal came for the assault. It was near noon when suddenly three rockets leaped high in the air, and a crash of musketry notified that the French had opened the ball on the right. " Forward the stormers," cried the General commanding the attack. "Forward," cried the Colonels of the leading regiments. " Away there the ladder party," shouted an officer of Engineers. The bugles rang out the charge. " Forward —th," shouted Hugh Fleming, as he and Byng sprang over the parapet, and dashed forward at a steady double straight for the salient of the great Redan, while the very heavens resounded with the sharp rattle of musketry from all sides. The *abattis* was broken rapidly by the Sappers in three or four places, but even that momentary delay occasioned fearful havoc in the ranks of the assailants, while the Rússian batteries now swept the space between their own lines and the British right attack with a murderous cross fire of grape and canister. Still they pressed on, dauntless as ever, though now at every step a man pitched forward and rolled over. What is left of the two leading regiments, the sailors and Sappers, have gained the ditch of the Redan. Byng sprang into the ditch, closely followed by his men; two or three of the Engineers promptly raised a ladder; he rushed towards it and a terrible malediction escaped his lips as he discovered that it was too short. A little to his right Hugh Fleming has been more fortunate, and having cleared a space by the free use of his revolver, has gained the parapet. His men swarm up after him. A sharp hand-to-hand fight, and the salient of the Redan is won! Up other ladders their comrades pour to their assistance, and slowly but steadily the foe is driven back to the gorge of the work.

But where are the reinforcements? They have room now to use plenty of men if they had them, but they are too weak in numbers to follow their foe further than they have already driven him. This the enemy is not slow to perceive; he rallies and stands his ground. The opposing parties pause, and glare at each other like pugilists between the rounds, when the battle is far from foughten out. But there is this terrible difference between them ; whereas no reinforcements are reaching the English, they are steadily pouring in to the Russians.

The gallant Colonel who leads the stormers is beside himself with vexation. He has won the work—is he to lose it, and all the lives it has cost him be wasted in vain ? Messenger after messenger he dispatches in search of those sorely-needed reinforcements, but they never come back.

" Look here ! " he said, addressing a small knot of officers who had temporarily gathered near the parapet, " do I look as if I was in a funk ? "

" Not a bit more than the rest of us, sir," promptly replied a captain of the Light Division.

" Well," he continued, " reinforcements I must have if I am to hold this work. I've sent four messengers for them, not one of them has returned nor have the reinforcements come. Now, gentlemen, I'm going myself, and if anything happens to me, I trust to you to do justice to my memory, and testify that I didn't go into that infernal cross fire because *I was afraid,*" and in another moment he had leapt over the parapet, and was gone.

He did not share the fate of his messengers, but like them, he never returned. Before he could obtain the reinforcements he went for, the Russians had swept the English out of the Redan and driven them back pell-mell to their own trenches.

It was the lull before the storm, the officers took advantage of the respite to reform and steady their men, to slip fresh cartridges into their revolvers, and generally to brace themselves for the coming struggle. They could see fresh troops pouring in to the assistance of their opponents, they knew that the strife between them must be renewed in a few minutes, and unless aid came to them, and that soon, they knew well what the result of that strife must be. Not a man wavered, not a cheek blanched, they knew what they had to do—to hold that work as long as they could and then die.

The pause is soon over ; cheered on by their officers, and exultant in their replenished numbers, with a wild yell, the Russians once more hurl themselves on the foe ; dauntlessly are they met, and one of those savage hand-to-hand melées in which men's eyes, like the Chourineur's in Sue's famous novel, see blood, ensues. Bayonet thrusts, and furious blows with clubbed muskets, are exchanged on all sides.   In the midst of this very whirlpool of battle Private Phybbs, still sticking close to Hugh's heels, with the canine fidelity he had displayed during the entire morning, found himself immersed. The confused mass swayed backwards and forwards when suddenly there came a final rush on the part of the Muscovites, and, by sheer weight of numbers, the English were driven rapidly back. Peter Phybbs was doing his *devoir* gallantly in the fray, when just as this retrograde movement began, his foot slipped on the blood-stained soil, and, at the same moment, he received a blow from the butt-end of a musket on the shoulder, which brought him to the ground. Another moment, and the bayonet of a powerful Russian Grenadier would have terminated the career of the luckless soldier, when a bullet from Hugh's revolver stretched the Grenadier across the legs of his intended victim. For a few moments Fleming made a gallant stand and, with the aid of his death-dealing revolver, kept his foes at bay. At length, hurling the empty pistol furiously in their faces, he was about to fall back, when a bayonet thrust in the side caused him to reel backwards, and before he could recover himself he was in the fierce grip of his foremost foes. Short had been his shrift, perhaps, for the blood of his assailants was up, and they had seen two or three of their comrades fall by his hand, but luckily for Hugh, one of their officers was close by, and sternly commanded that his life should be spared. But to this, having fainted from loss of blood, Hugh was utterly oblivious.

If those few moments have cost Hugh Fleming his life, they have undoubtedly saved that of Peter Phybbs. But for Hugh's revolver, his spirit would have already sped, but Fleming's stand had enabled him to recover his feet, rejoin his comrades, and be with them swept over the parapet by the victorious wave of Russian troops. As for the broken and defeated remnant of the English, they tumbled pell-mell into the ditch of the Redan, as Tom Byng described it afterwards, " like detected schoolboys over an orchard wall," and made their way back to their own lines by twos and threes, and without any attempt at formation. If they had strewn the ground thick as leaves in Autumn, during their advance, it is certain that they suffered but little in their retreat. Whether the Russian batteries deemed it probable that their troops, following up the success they had gained, might make a sortie in force, or whether they chivalrously abstained from further punishment of a thoroughly beaten foe, I cannot say, but so it was, and both Byng and Private Phybbs were amongst those who regained the advanced trench comparatively unhurt. Over Hugh Fleming's fate his comrades could only shake their heads sadly when they got back to the camp. He had never been seen after that last charge of the Russians, which had swept them out of the Redan, and in all probability he was numbered with the slain. It seemed to his comrades the very irony of fate to read in the general orders for the army that evening :

" Lieutenant Hugh Fleming, —th Regiment, to be Lieutenant and Captain in the Grenadier Guards. Captain Fleming will report himself at once to the Quarter-Master General with regard to his passage for England."

END OF VOL I.

www.ingramcontent.com/pod-product-compliance
Lightning Source LLC
Chambersburg PA
CBHW031427020726
47499CB00005B/1629